THE BETRAYAL

LJ Byrne

ISBN-13: 9798661223296
ISBN-10: 1477123456

Cover design by: Art Painter
Library of Congress Control Number: 2018675309
Printed in the United States of America

CONTENTS

PROLOGUE

Five years ago…

My father looms over me. "Do you remember everything you are to say?" he demands. Lionel Atherton is a severe man. He hates to be disappointed.

"Yes, Father," I say, keeping my eyes lowered. I am clean, dressed in a pinstriped blue dress. "I left bed at eight because I was thirsty. I saw Blake Remington leave Father's library. His clothes were messy. He didn't see me. I heard someone crying in the library, but I was scared so I went back into my room."

"Do not disappoint me," he tells me, patting his belt meaningfully. He exchanges a glance with my oldest brother, Brett.

I can hardly move, but when the detective arrives, Father tells me to sit down. Tears come to my eyes as I sit down slowly. The detective is a nice-looking man, and he has a kind face. Mother brings him in and offers him tea.

"It would be best if I spoke to her alone," the detective says, "but as she's a minor, maybe her mother could stay?"

Lionel Atherton does not like to be questioned, but he looks at my mother and nods. He and Brett leave, and Mother sits next to me, her hand on my back.

"Laura," the detective asks me very gently, "do you know Blake Remington?"

I nod. My mother's fingers dig into my back and I start weeping. "Yes."

"How do you know him?" The detective hands me tissues.

"He's Rory's big brother," I whisper.

"Rory Remington?"

"Yes. He's best friends with my brother."

"Which brother, Laura?"

"Jin, my twin brother."

"Can you tell me what you saw Saturday night? Your father said you were put to bed early."

Do not say anything but what you are to say. I tell the detective what my father told me to say. My mother looks on in cold approval.

I have a bad feeling I've done something wrong. I want Jin, but I know the rules. When I answer the remaining questions, my mother's hand is my reminder. My tears are not fake.

LAURA

CHAPTER 1

Jin is being sent to military school. My parents announce this to us one evening over dinner. We are never given a chance to discuss the matter. When it comes to either of us, compliance is assumed.

My father, Lionel Atherton, is not a man of conversation. At an early age, I learned that his paternal responsibility is to assure a roof over our table and food. Beyond that, I am on my own. He is in his late forties and still looks strong for his age. We are the eternal source of discontent.

"Because of your sister, you have become weak, Jin. Military school will make a man out of you," he says. "You will not be coming home frequently as I wish to see progress."

Beneath the table, my twin reaches for my hand and squeezes. But to our father, he shows no reaction. "Yes, Father."

My oldest brother, Brett, gives his younger brother a sneer. "Just don't come home gay or something. I'd had to beat faggots out of you." He laughs like he thinks this is funny. Both Jin and I look at him blankly. We are careful not to react.

You think I'd kill my little sister? What kind of monster do you think I am?

This is a house of horror and comedy. We are the actors being forced on stage to endure this mockery of a home.

My mother, still very beautiful and still very vain, shakes her head. "Oh, Brett, you shouldn't tease your brother. He might improve, after all." There is a wistfulness in her voice, but when she addresses me, there is only disapproval. "I will expect you to be twice as helpful, Laura."

Jin squeezes my hand again under the table. *You'll be okay. We'll be okay.* We communicate without words.

"I'm going to a club, Dad," Brett says. He is the only one who calls our father 'Dad'. He is the favorite son. Handsome. Cruel. Barely controllable. My father nods benevolently.

When Mother and Brett leave the table, my father pins his eyes on me. "While your brother is away, I expect you to conduct yourself honorably. You don't want to become a whore, do you? Do you understand me?"

"Yes, Father."

"Look at me when I talk to you."

I raise my eyes. My shoulders tremble, but Jin squeezes my hands. *I'm here. We'll be okay.*

"I've noticed your clothes are becoming too tight again." My father twists his mouth. "It's disgusting the way you expose yourself."

I am wearing a long-sleeved t-shirt and sweats. This is approved attire. "I—I don't understand."

"From now on, I want you to wear hoodies on top. I won't have boys thinking they can have their way with you. I've asked your mother to go to a discount store and find something appropriate."

All my clothes come from the discount store. We're not poor, but it is a waste of money to buy me anything new. Brett gets into a lot of trouble; we're frequently paying people to keep him out of trouble.

"You two are excused. Jin, you leave in the morning."

My eyes grow wide. I gasp.

"Your mother's relatives will let you stay with them until school begins," my father continues, smiling at us. He sees my brother flinch. This causes Father to get upset. "Don't act like a girl, Jin. Now leave. Both of you."

I go to Jin's room. My twin pulls me into his arms. "It'll be okay. Just one more year. Then, we'll be eighteen. I'll take you away from here, I promise. I'll take you somewhere safe."

When I start crying, he continues. "I'll work several jobs, and we'll go to community college. We'll take care of each other. I'll buy you a dress." He's quiet as he rocks me. "I've done a poor job of protecting you. When we're eighteen, they can't do anything to stop us."

This is our favorite game. We imagine a life free from this home, free from our parents.

"We'll do a video chat every night while you're gone," I whisper. "They can't stop that."

"I'll find a way to take care of you, Ara." He uses my nickname lovingly. "I promise."

It is because we have each other that we know how to love. We are father, mother, brother, sister to each other. In our sibling bond, we rationalize and learn about the world, about how people should be. We survive because we have each other.

Both of us know that the separation is part cruelty, part punishment. Jin has not turned out the way that Father wants. Although we are obedient, we lack the drive, we lack the coldness.

In the morning, my parents don't let me go with them to the airport. They force me to stay home while Jin is taken from me. I stand by my bedroom window as the car is driven away.

I'm isolated and alone. Just the way my parents like it. I sit down on my bed and wait.

"Hello. Would you like to be our friend?"

"I don't have any friends here."

"We're not allowed to have many friends. It makes perfect sense to have a friend who doesn't have any friends. That way, I'll never have to worry about having too many friends."

We stand in the courtyard, the three of us. It's cold, and I have my hood pulled close around my face. Jin extends his hand. The other boy takes it. When the other boy looks at me, I shiver. His eyes are the most glorious blue I've ever seen.

CHAPTER 2

Jin and I talk every night. Our relatives are nicer than Mother and Father, but he's careful with his words. He never disparages in case word gets back to our parents to cause me harm. He tells me that our cousins think he's pretty handsome for a half-Korean and we laugh. I miss his presence and spend most of the day avoiding Brett, who's frequently in a bad mood, and Father. It's important to stay guarded against Brett.

I'm cleaning the toilets when Brett finds me. In sweats and a hooded sweatshirt, I am a gray lump. "Hey, loser, Dad wants you in his library."

I flinch. I hate Father's library. *I left bed at eight because I was thirsty. I saw Blake Remington leave Father's library. His clothes were messy. He didn't see me. I heard someone crying in the library, but I was scared so I went back into my room.*

Brett follows me, breathing heavily. Sometimes he walks too close in a form of psychological terror. Other times, he puts his hand on my shoulder as a reminder of the violence he could inflict at will. I try to control the pounding of my heart as I enter the library. My father, holding a glass of cognac, watches me with dead eyes as I come in. My mother is perched near him, her bottom on the desk. But the person who grabs my attention is a thin woman in a fashionable pink suit seated in an upholstered chair.

My mother, her face bright with too much makeup, peers at me sharply. "Laura, come say hello to your Aunt Clara."

Aunt Clara is Father's older sister. She rises slowly. The only resemblance I see between the two of them are the eyes. They have the same hazel eyes. Aunt Clara is shorter, her bones more severe, and there is slight gauntness to her features.

"This is her, then," Aunt Clara says, examining me like I'm a rug she's going to buy. "Is she healthy, Hae?"

"Oh, yes. Very healthy. Strong, too." My mother nods her heads in excitement. I wonder if I should let her examine my teeth.

My aunt looks at me. "I'm offering your father the deal of a lifetime, Laura. My cancer has returned. I don't want servants cleaning up after me. If he lets me have you while I undergo treatment again, and you do a good job taking care of me, when I die, I will leave my money to you and your father."

"Why to her? I'm the oldest," Brett complains. "Don't I deserve money, too?"

Mother soothes him, "Never worry, Brett. Of course, you do."

My aunt doesn't mince words. "If you want to clean up my vomit and my waste, I'll give you money, too."

Brett makes a face and goes silent.

"Well, Lionel? I'm worth a lot of money," she says in a cold voice. "What say you?"

My eyes widen. Holy cow.

The greedy gleam in my father's eyes sickens me. He'd sell me to sex traffickers if he could. "I don't see why Laura gets the money since she's my daughter," my father says, and my mother nods emphatically. "Why, we're doing you a favor! It should all come to me."

Aunt Clara narrows her eyes. "I have no children. I will have no children. She does a good job and that is her reward." She pulls out a check. "This is for one million dollars. Sort of a prepayment if you accept my terms. My doctors tell me my prognosis isn't great. I'll cover her education while she's with me, of course."

Mother snatches the check quickly. "Lionel, this is a good thing for everyone. I think the deal – it's a good one."

Brett makes a sound of distaste, his dark eyes glaring at me.

But Father agrees with Mother. "How soon do you want her?"

I see the similarity between my father and aunt when Aunt Clara says, "Have her ready to leave in less than half an hour. I hate waiting. My plane takes off soon."

Mother helps me pack, all the while telling me to be thankful for my good fortune. "Don't make your aunt angry. Do everything she says. Don't eat too much food. Do not be lazy. Clean up after yourself. Don't speak unless you have to. If you ruin this for our family, you will be punished severely."

I'll protect you from the dark, I promise, Ara. Nothing bad will happen

I ignore the voice from my past, staying silent and nodding. I send Jin a text, so he knows that something is happening. My mother packs three pairs of sweats, underwear, long-sleeved shirts, and hoodies. It's summer and I'm dressed like it's fifty degrees outside.

I pack my phone, a few pencils, and grab the stuffed bunny that Jin won for me when we were twelve. There are no hugs, no tears, no good wishes. I glance at the two-story building which was supposed to be a home with almost no emotion.

Outside, my aunt has a black car waiting. "Hurry and get in. I want to be home as soon as possible," she barks.

I bend my head meekly and shuffle inside the car. I glance at my parents. Both are smiling. Brett glares at me, his mouth twisted in a frown. I wonder how long it will be before I see them again. I don't feel any pangs as they disappear from view.

My aunt is quiet for the entire drive to the local airport. I've never been on a private plane before, which makes me wonder how much my aunt is worth.

I try to make myself as small as possible.

At the airport, I gawk at the plane for a bit. A man with a hat takes my bag and carries it on the plane for me. I follow my aunt onto the plane, and she gestures to a chair.

She takes the seat across from me and only then does she sigh and relax. An attendant comes by. "Mary, get me a drink. And get this girl some food. She looks like a skeleton."

I hastily buckle myself in.

"What are you wearing, girl?" Aunt Clara asks irritably. "It's eighty-five degrees and you're in sweats. Do you only own things that are gray?"

"I'm sorry."

"What for?" Aunt Clara snaps but then looks away.

Food is brought to me. A sandwich. Some chips. A bottle of water and orange juice. My aunt is handed a glass of brown liquid.

"Thank you, Aunt Clara."

"Call me Clara."

"Yes, Clara."

Her sharp eyes come to a decision, but I don't know what. "Where's your twin brother?"

"Jin is in California attending military school."

"Humph. Eat up. I'm taking a nap after I finish this. Don't bother me."

"Yes, A – Clara."

I spend the rest of the trip eating slowly and thoughtfully with my future looming before me with uncertainty.

CHAPTER 3

It's late when we land on the East Coast. I barely remember the drive. I think I'm carried into the home, but I drift into a dreamless sleep. In the morning, when I wake, it's because my phone is buzzing. It's Jin texting me with concern.

I write back and we make plans to talk in a few hours. Then I look around, confused. I must be in the guest bedroom because it's far too sumptuous and big. It's a nice bed, done in neutral tones, and it has a good plush feel. A polite knock heralds the arrival of a gray-haired woman.

"Hello, I'm Ellen, may I come in?"

Ellen looks to be about fifty. Her features are plain but kind. She's dressed smartly in one of those pantsuits in olive green. "You look well-rested," she says with a smile. "I'm your aunt's personal assistant – and sort of a house-keeper. Now, come stand up."

I stand up, puzzled, as she measures me from head to toe, typing a few things into her tablet.

"Where am I to sleep?" I ask.

Ellen frowns. "Here. This is your bedroom, dear. Your bathroom is fully stocked, and I'll have fresh clothes for you this afternoon. We didn't know your size, but I'm going to remedy all of that right now."

"What? Where is my aunt?" The panic must be evident in my voice because Ellen gently pats my back.

"There, dear. Be calm. I don't know much about you, but your aunt said I was to be gentle with you and that you've been through a lot. Your aunt is under-going treatment right now. She'll be back later."

"But I'm supposed to go with her and take care of her!"

Ellen frowns even more. "My dear, we have nurses for that," she says like I just said something silly. "I was told that you are to rest and get acquainted. Let me get the orders in for your clothes, and I'll come and talk to you further. You start school soon, and we'll need to get your uniforms ready to go."

"Uniforms?" My head is spinning. Maybe I'm dreaming because none of this can be real.

"Why don't you freshen up, and I'll meet you in the kitchen?" Ellen suggests kindly. "I can walk you through everything you need to know. There's a good chance you won't see Clara very much today."

After Ellen leaves, I call Jin. He listens quietly and then advises me to observe and be on my toes. I try not to cry when I hear his voice so full of compassion. *Be strong, you twit*, I chide myself.

Ellen was right: the bathroom is fully stocked with a brand-new electric toothbrush and even face wash. I do my best to look neat and presentable, changing my clothes and folding my dirty ones into a neat pile.

I get lost looking for the kitchen, but someone wiping the windows notices me and directs me. I pass through several rooms, some quite cavernous. Why does one woman need such a large home?

When I get to the kitchen, a round-faced man named Stefan smiles at me. "Ah, there's my diner," he says, pulling out a plate from the oven. "Sit, sit. The plate's hot. I wasn't sure what kind of girl you'd be, but most people like my blueberry pancakes."

I stare at the plate. I usually just have toast in the morning.

"What's wrong? Are you vegan? Please don't tell me you're vegan," he groans.

"I'm not vegan," I whisper, my eyes huge as I stare at the plate of food.

He sighs in relief. "Excellent. Coffee, tea, hot chocolate?"

I work on breakfast, wondering how in the world I'm supposed to eat this much, with Stefan singing in the background and plying me with hot chocolate. It's cheerful in a surreal kind of way. He explains that Aunt Clara eats an extremely specific diet so he's prepping meals for her – tiny ones – in hopes she can keep something down. I'm riddled with guilt. I'm supposed to take care of her, right?

Ellen finds me just as I think I'm about to explode from eating. "Oh, good. Stefan fed you. Alright, you seem pretty confused so let me explain what you're doing here."

I put my hands politely in my lap to listen.

"In two weeks, you'll be starting at Cove Preparatory Academy as a third-year student," Ellen begins like this is a normal conversation. "I know you have a driver's license, so you'll use the Range Rover. Not the fanciest vehicle but drives well in winter weather. It has GPS, too. We got your high school records, and you've been assigned classes accordingly. Your uniforms will be here next week, and your wardrobe should be mostly done today. I have a credit card for you to buy anything we missed." She hands me a credit card that has my name on it.

"Clara brought me here to take care of her," I say stupidly, and Stefan pauses to glance at me in surprise.

Ellen just smiles. "On weekends, if Clara feels good, you can read to her. She likes being read to. Other than that, I recommend you stay out of her way. She gets temperamental at times. When you're hungry, just tell Stefan. There are usually things in the fridge for you to eat, and you can tell Stefan what you like to keep on hand. Any questions?"

My hands are shaking. "What am I supposed to do?" This is not what I expected.

Stefan and Ellen exchange a look. "I've had your computer and other devices that teens like to have delivered to your room. Maybe you can set those up so they're ready to go. Get familiar with the house. Go for a drive." She looks at my clothes. "You may wish to change your clothes. Clara would not want people to see you dressed like that."

Shame rises to my face. "What should I wear? I mean, are long-sleeved shirts okay?"

The older woman's brows come together. "You can wear whatever you like, my dear. This is your home. I'm sure Clara wants you to feel comfortable." A buzz on her phone alerts her and she checks messages. "Ah, I had them fill your closet with basics and they're here." She sends a message back. "Come, let me show you."

I pick up my plate and head towards the sink, biting my lip because I'm not sure if I should wash them now or later. Stefan carefully removes the items from my hands. "I'll take that, sweetie pie. You don't need to do dishes."

Ellen just steers me back to my room where I find boxes and bags stacked on the bed. Without pausing, Ellen does this weird inventory check. "Laptop. iPad. Oh, your new phone. Your current one would be mocked at Cove Prep. I've already activated your phone." She points to the boxes. "Just a few dresses and some shoes." Her eyes glance at my worn sneakers. "There should be underwear and accessories in one of these bags. You seem like a basics kind of girl, so mostly just jeans, some tops."

"I'm not supposed to wear jeans," I whisper, and Ellen laughs like she thinks I'm joking, but then she stops when she sees the expression on my face.

"My dear, you can wear jeans here," she says softly. "In fact, I think you might look very nice in some of these clothes. I have to get things ready for Clara when she returns from treatment, but I'll check in on you before I leave, alright?"

I nod, trying not to cry. When I'm finally alone, I call Jin. "I am having a really weird day," I begin. And then I unload on my twin.

CHAPTER 4

The school uniform fits well. Too well. I stare at my legs in dismay. They're *showing.* The skirt ends right above the knee even though I try to pull it down further. The white shirt is fitted, and you can see the curve of my breasts even with the jacket on. The black silk tie just seems to draw attention to the fact that I have breasts. This is not a good thing!

I'm literally having a mini-panic attack. If Father sees me like this, he'll be furious. But then I realize that Father and Mother (and Brett) aren't here. That calms me enough to finish my hair and put my shoes on. Is it wrong to feel relief at being away from my family? Is it wrong to feel a touch of excitement at seeing my legs? When I look again in the mirror, I bite my lip to stop my smile. I think it looks cute.

A week ago, Ellen sent me to get my hair cut. I've never had it professionally cut before. Mother usually cuts it with hair shears. The woman wanted to do all sorts of crazy things with my hair because she said it lacked style. I end up with a slightly shorter do that goes to the middle of my back with some layers. It's still pretty simple.

I've only seen Clara a few times since my arrival. My first weekend, she did invite me to read to her. I read *Great Expectations* to her until she fell asleep. I know that she was quite ill after her round of chemotherapy, but the nurse handled everything. I offered to help, but Ellen shooed me away and told me to eat something.

Stefan gives me the local gossip about the school over breakfast. Lots of fancy cars and lots of fancy parties. It sounds intimidating. Usually, I have Jin with me, but this is the first time I've gone to school by myself. I practiced the route to Cove Prep so on the first day of school, I'm completely prepared.

I park the Range Rover carefully – Father is particular about how cars are parked – and step out with my bookbag. I remember Stefan's words about fancy cars, and he isn't wrong. The parking lot is littered with high-end, luxury vehicles.

A silver Aston Martin parks next to me, and I make the mistake of glancing at the driver. The color drains from my face. I would recognize him anywhere.

Rory Remington steps out of his car, his face livid and pale. "You!" he spits out, hate in his eyes. "What the fuck are you doing here?" He takes in my uniform. "No way. You are *not* a student here!"

I last saw Rory five years ago. He's taller – like over six feet tall. He's grown handsome, muscular. The youthful features are more angular, but his eyes are the same – the vivid blue that fascinated me the first time we met. He storms around his car, practically lunging at me.

I cringe against the Range Rover, flinching when he slams one hand against the car.

"Why are you here?!" he demands, grabbing my arm roughly with the other hand.

"My aunt lives nearby," I whisper. "She's sending me here."

Disgust fills his eyes as he looks at me, at my designer shoes, and then at the car I'm driving. "Little Laura Atherton has grown up, but she's still the little bitch she was five years ago." He lowers his voice. "Where's Jin?"

I'm literally shaking in my shoes. "Not here," I breathe. "He's at another school."

"Aww, no one to protect you," Rory says with malicious glee. "Can't hide behind your brothers now, can you?" I blink at him. "You made a huge mistake coming here. I am going to make your life hell for what you did to Blake with your lying mouth. I will ruin you at this school. You'll know what it is to be hated."

He pushes me away roughly, looming over me when I fall to the ground. I hold back my tears. I think he's about to say something, but he stops, spitting at the ground, and walks off.

Shaken, I crouch on the ground for a few minutes. He hates me. And I can't say I blame him.

"Come on, Ara, we don't want to miss the rocket launch." Jin grabs my hand. We're twelve and I hate that he's taller than me.

When we get there, I can't see a thing. I can barely see the setup on my tippy toes. Rory tugs on his older brother's arm, gesturing to me. Blake is five years older and I have a silly schoolgirl crush on him. He's tall and handsome. I blink when the Remington brothers reach us.

"Don't worry, Ara," Rory says, using my brother's nickname for me, taking my hand gently. "We'll help you."

Both Rory and Jin have gone through a growth spurt, but I'm still short. Blake swings me up onto his shoulders so I can see over the crowd. I look down to see my twin and Rory staring at me, both smiling at my happiness. My face is flustered. For a moment, I forget all the bad things around me. I don't think about my father or Brett. I feel like a queen.

What I did was unforgivable. Perhaps this is my punishment, my time to atone. I can't go back in time and undo the past. People were hurt and I'm too blame. Rory's hatred is justified, and if he is hell-bent on revenge, who's to say I don't deserve it?

My twin's handsome face scowls. "What do you mean Rory Remington is at your new school?" he asks as if it wasn't a certainty. "What did he say?"

I don't tell him the threats. I just tell him that Rory said he hated me.

Jin tries to gauge if I'm holding something back. "He probably hates both of us. But, Ara, if he does something cruel to you, will you tell me? Whatever you do, don't mention it to Father. Or to Brett."

My laugh is bitter. "Do you think I have daily chats with either of them? I wouldn't mention it to them even if I did."

"I always wanted to reach out to them," Jin muses aloud. "But what could we say without risk?" We fall silent. Then anxiously, Jin says, "There's so much to do once we're free. You'll see."

"What if Father says that I'm—"

Jin interrupts me sharply. "Don't say it! You know it isn't true. I've failed you most of my life. I won't do it again. It will *never* happen."

"You've never failed me. We're trapped." I hug myself.

Jin and I share one of those twin looks – it's where we say a dozen things just by sharing a look. Finally, he says, "I like your uniform. You look nice."

I blush. "I'm still getting used to seeing my legs. I don't see Aunt Clara a lot. It's a little weird not having someone lurking in the background." I glance around my room. "I'm scared of getting used to it."

"I know exactly what you mean."

On the last day of school, Rory, Jin, and I walk slowly home. Jin and I aren't in a rush to be home, and Rory seems happy just being with us. Jin and I take each other's hands and dance beneath a large tree. Rory watches us for a few minutes before tapping on Jin's shoulder. He bows to me. I pretend to curtsey. He takes my hand and twirls me as we dance. Jin watches, his smile knowing.

CHAPTER 5

The next day at school, I get a taste of what life will be like. The first day, I was largely ignored. The second day, I notice several students whispering when they glance at me. I keep my head down. If I don't look at them, no one can escalate. In the hallway, a boy bumps roughly into me.

I mutter an apology, but the boy grabs me and pushes me against the wall. I freeze. He's taller than me – I'm not that short – but he's huge for a teen. Steroids? "You're Laura, right?" he asks, and I don't like the way his left hand pins me to the wall while his right hand is at my waist.

"I didn't mean to bump into you," I whisper.

"You're pretty. A little too skinny, but not too bad." He cups my bottom. "Rory said you were easy on the eyes and easy in bed."

I feel like throwing up. "Wh-what?" I squeak, trying to push his hands off.

"How about you show me what Midwest girls can do?"

I start to struggle. I hate how weak I am. I hate how ineffective I am. The students passing by us pretend to be oblivious as he gropes me. "No."

"Hey, jackass, get your hands off her!"

The boy turns to see a tall, athletic girl. "Go away, Emily. I'm having a bit of fun."

Emily tosses her brown hair back. "It looks like sexual assault to me. I saw her say no, Dario."

Dario grunts, his hand still at my throat. Behind Emily, Rory walks with a girl on his arm. He stops smiling. When Dario drops his hand to my thigh, like he's about to go under my skirt, my eyes widen in terror. I start scratching and fighting in earnest. Like a tiger, Emily joins the fray and jumps on Dario's back. He throws her off, his hold on my throat tightening.

"Get your hands off her!" Rory snaps, his voice cutting through the voices of students watching and doing nothing. The girl at his side pouts as he shrugs her off and moves forward.

Dario actually drops his hands, and I slump to the floor. "Just having a bit of fun, Rory. You told me she was easy."

Rory's face darkens with rage, fists clenched, but before he can speak, another boy appears. He's broader than Dario. And huge. "Did you touch my sister, Dario? Why the fuck is my sister on the floor?" His voice is quiet with menace.

Emily sneers at Dario. "He threw me, Kenji, when I tried to help this girl. He was touching her without her permission. And then the asshole threw me."

Kenji cracks his knuckles, and his calmness makes the knuckle bit even more terrifying. "Everyone knows my sister is off-limits. Everyone knows you don't touch my sister. If she tells you to leave someone alone, you really need to listen to her." He speaks quietly, but the students give him space. "Come, Dario, you and I must talk."

I glance around, my tear-stained face meeting Rory's indecipherable one. Kenji grabs Dario, and I'm surprised to see the boy blubbering apologies as he's dragged away. Emily extends a hand to me. "I'm Emily Takemono. We're in some of the same classes. I recognize you from yesterday. Come on. Let me help you up."

With her help, I stand shakily. I can't imagine how pathetic I must look. As we walk past Rory, he hisses, "Maybe you'll learn what it's like to be accused of something you didn't to."

I don't reply. Emily fishes around for a clean handkerchief. "Here. Mom always puts a clean one in my bag. She says it's a sign of a lady." Emily laughs. Her features are like mine with a mix of Asian and Caucasian features – she's probably half-Japanese like how I'm half-Korean. "I don't know what your history with Rory is, but he's one of the Idols and he's been telling a lot of stories about you."

"Idols?"

"Yup. Rory, Jaylen, and Zyair. I think the rule is hot, rich, jerk. Paris, Stacy, and Deanna are their groupies." She ticks each name off on her finger. "My brother is a wrestler. We're not Idols, but no one screws with us because then you deal with Kenji. He's the state champion. He's a fourth-year so I lose him next year, but I'm no lightweight myself. Paris was the girl on Rory's arm. She's a major bitch and the epitome of Mean Girls." Her eyes flicker over me. "No need to introduce yourself. As the new girl, we know your name, and Rory's made sure people know a ton of stuff about you."

I pale. "You don't have to help me. I appreciate the kindness."

Emily shrugs. "I make my own decisions. Kenji says I'm stubborn that way. The way Rory talks make me think he has a grudge. People with grudges aren't always honest."

I hold my tongue. I'm a coward. I should tell her that I deserve it. I deserve all of it.

"You've never seen fireflies at night before?" Rory asks, glancing at me in surprise.

Jin grabs my hand and squeezes. "I go to bed at eight," I say quietly. "Father says it's important to get enough rest."

"Sneak out tonight. Both of you," Rory urges, grabbing my other hand and swinging it. "I'll meet you at nine." He looks expectantly at both of us. "It'll be an adventure."

"Father will be angry if he finds out," I whisper, but Rory shrugs.

Jin looks at me and then at his best friend. "We could try," he hedges.

Rory kisses the back of my hand. "I'll protect you from the dark, I promise, Ara. Nothing bad will happen."

"Okay." Only Jin hears the tremor of my voice.

Emily keeps up a constant, cheerful chatter and I miss her presence when we part after our first two classes. Unfortunately, Rory is in my math class. He ignored me yesterday, but today, his eyes gleam with malicious intent.

"I've told everyone that you're prone to diseases," he sneers after sitting behind me. "Wouldn't want anyone to get dirty from touching you." He yanks on my hair hard when I don't say anything. Tears spring to my eyes. "I'm talking to you, bitch."

I realize he wants me to respond. "I heard you."

"Don't give me that innocent voice," he hisses behind me. "We all know you're a snake and a liar." He pauses. "How could you do it, Laura? How could you do that to Blake? He was always nice to you. How could you do that to me?"

For a moment, I hear his vulnerability. I don't turn around.

"I thought we were friends," he continues, his voice becoming hard.

"I'm sorry," I whisper.

"Sorry doesn't cut it. I thought you were special. But now, I know you're just like your father. You'll do anything so your family wins, including sending an innocent person to jail." This time he yanks on my hair harder. "You're lucky it didn't go to court. Lying under oath is a crime."

It didn't go to court because Marigold Summers refused to testify, refused to admit anything. But there was a crime. She was a victim. And the person who did it got away. Because of me.

"I've set the girls on you." He laughs. "We'll see if you survive the year. Maybe you'll do us a favor and go away all on your own."

I think about Aunt Clara and my reasons for being here. I'm away from Brett and Father. That's something, right? I don't care about the money. In fact, if it means they'll leave me alone, they can have every penny. I know Jin wants to go to medical school. I'll find a way to make that happen. I'll find a way to atone for all my sins.

I'm given a reprieve when the teacher starts the class. But I'm left with one incontrovertible truth: no one can protect me from the dark.

CHAPTER 6

Emily and Kenji allow me to join them for lunch every day. I don't know if Emily's aware that, by doing so, she stops a lot of horrible things from happening to me in the lunchroom. Honestly, I remain clueless until a whole cup of iced tea is dumped on me the moment Emily and Kenji leave.

From their table, the Idols point and laugh at me as Paris elegantly empties her cup over my head. I don't react – I've perfected this because the punishment was always worse if I protested or tried to protect Jin. Rory stands and smirks at me as Paris returns to his side. Some of the students throw napkins at me until the staff intervenes. I don't look at anyone as I walk to the restroom to dry off as best as I can.

When I get home, Ellen finds me desperately trying to wash the tea stains out in the sink. She takes the ruined clothes from my hands gently, telling me not to cry over spilled tea with a wink, and sends me down to get something to eat. My hands shake as I worry that Aunt Clara will be angry that I've spoiled perfectly good clothes.

Stefan puts a chunk of bread in front of me with a bowl of soup. "Eat up, kid, you look like you need it," he says but not unkindly. "You want to talk about your day?"

I shake my head. "I just had an accident," I whisper.

"It's pretty lonely in this big house, isn't it? Maybe you should invite some of your new classmates," he suggests. "I can make a whole lot of food."

My eyes grow wide. "No. No, I don't do parties. I don't – my father doesn't like for me to socialize too much because there are a lot of negative influences out there."

Stefan regards me quietly. "Kid, your father isn't here. I don't see anything wrong with maybe having a pizza party."

Nothing wrong except people hate me. I shake my head. "I'm just going to stay focused on my studies. Do well in school so I can get a good job, you know." I bite into my bread. It's fresh. Homemade. My hands shake

Stefan doesn't say anything. "Well, if you change your mind, just know I love to cook, bake, and talk."

I blink back tears. I don't deserve kindness, but I crave it. I want someone to hold me and tell me it will get better. I scold myself. *Vile, weak, pathetic.*

After dinner, Ellen stops by to tell me that Aunt Clara wants to see me. When I enter her room, there's a nice male nurse who places a chair close to the bed. Aunt Clara is pale, her skin puffy from the treatments. There's soup in front of her, too, but it looks different from what I ate earlier. The nurse is helping her sip it slowly. The room smells of sickness and antiseptic. Even with the cheerful bed patterns and bright lights, there's a pall over everything.

"Come closer, Laura," my aunt rasps, gesturing to a book of poems. "Read to me while I eat."

"Of course, Clara." I sit by the bed and start reading, trying to keep my voice calm and soothing. After about twenty minutes, she has me stop.

"Do you have everything you need for school?" Clara asks.

"Yes, thank you. I – I appreciate your generosity, but I feel like I should be doing something more than reading." I look around the room. "I can clean toilets and do the windows if you like."

My aunt's pale eyes flicker. "I didn't bring you here to be my maid." Her frame is still small despite the puffiness of her body and face. "Do you think I was blind? No teen girl walks around in the summer heat in sweats. Do you think I don't know my brother? He was born a control freak. Him and your mother. All she cares is about her beauty. She'll let your father do anything as long as she can pamper herself." She mutters for a bit. "You know, he only wanted sons. No girls. But fate decided to deny him that. You think I didn't see your face. You think I don't know what my brother did to his own daughter? What he let his son do?"

I lose all color in my face.

"I know. I saw. I held my tongue. But now I'm probably going to die." Her breath wheezes out. "Maybe I can save you. Maybe. Maybe you and Jin will be okay. Maybe I should have done something sooner. I doubted I could do much. You remember your blood. You are your father's daughter. But you also have my blood. No man. No man put me down." She coughs. "People can help you, but you must grab the bull by the horns. Do you understand me?"

"Yes," I say, but it's a lie. I don't understand what she's talking about. She seems distressed. I take her hand. "For whatever it's worth, I am grateful. I don't deserve this—"

Her hand twists to clench mine fiercely. "You think anyone deserves anything? No one gets what they deserve. No, this is not about desserts. I know him. I know my brother." Her eyes close suddenly, her hand loosens. "I'm tired. Go. Go and be a high school student. Next time you visit me, I would like to see you in a dress. None of these sweats. I will have Ellen burn them all if you do. You will dress like a teenager, God help me."

The nurse signals to me that I should go. I quietly return the chair to the corner. Before I leave, I look back at my aunt's pale form, her frame sunken in the bed.

"She knows," I whisper to Jin later that night. "She knows about Father and Brett."

My twin puts his hand out as if he could touch me. I match his hand on the screen. "Is she trying to keep you safe?"

I nod. "I think so." Some of the worry seeps from Jin's face.

"That's good. That's good. How is school?"

"It's okay."

"That doesn't sound good."

"How is school for you?"

Jin shrugs. "It's not bad. It's okay. Kids are nice. Girls are pretty."

I giggle. "Is there a girl you like?"

"You trying to get rid of your brother already? Just remember, I'm older by ten minutes. I'm wiser." When I dissolve into laughter, he smiles. "You should laugh more. When I'm eighteen, I'm going to make sure you laugh every day." He stops and grows serious. "You know there's nothing wrong with you, right? You're not crazy."

"Maybe I should be. Aren't we all a little crazy?" I won't look at him as I say this. "I'm your Achilles' heel, Jin."

"Don't say that!" he snaps. "You're my twin, my other half. We're stronger together."

"I miss you," I say to him. "I miss you so much."

"I miss you, too. I love you, Ara. Don't ever forget it."

That night, I remember the fireflies.

Jin helps me climb down from the upper window. I see Rory holding slippers for us to wear. He wiggles his flashlight and I smile because the thrill of disobedience is something I've never felt before. I feel alive. I'm in my nightgown, but I don't care.

Rory takes us to the back of the house they're renting. The family is only here for a year and I'm already sad about them leaving. Rory then flashes his light into the darkness. And just like that, tiny sparks of light shine back. He repeats it and the little fireflies flash back.

I gasp. "It's so pretty, Rory. It's the prettiest thing I've ever seen." I grab his hand and smile at him. "Thank you."

Rory looks right at me. "I think I'm looking at the prettiest thing I've ever seen," he whispers. I know Jin hears, but my brother doesn't say anything. He doesn't look at Rory either.

We stand in the darkness, Jin looking at the fireflies, but Rory and I look at each other.

CHAPTER 7

I stare at my locker. It's covered with profanities, lurid drawings, and condoms. The students around me snicker. Yesterday, I was tripped, bruising my knees.

"Well, it looks like everyone knows what kind of girl you are," Paris Dumonte drawls, walking up to me. Stacy Fletcher and Deanna Evans flank her. She grabs my wrist, her painted nails digging into my skin. "Rory told me all about how you're the little girl who cries wolf. You accuse guys of being very, very bad just for attention." Her red lips smile. "What I don't understand is why any guy would want you… You're a pathetic piece of meat. But I guess with a bag over your head, some guys don't care." She brings her face close to mine. "Stop throwing yourself at Rory Remington. It's pathetic."

I frown. "I don't know what you're—"

She slaps me hard. "I'm the Queen Bitch. You don't speak to me unless I permit you, you got it?" She doesn't wait for me to react. "He told me all about how desperate you are in math class. It's disgusting." Her voice grows dangerously soft. "If you try anything again, I'll send a boy who wants to get laid. He's not very good at taking no for an answer, though."

She slams my head into my locker for good measure, and by the time my head clears, she and her friends are gone.

Emily can tell I'm upset, but she doesn't press me. Her eyes flicker over the mark on my cheek. "Hey, what are you doing this weekend?" she asks in between classes. "I was going to catch that new action flick. Want to go?"

I blink at her. "I'm not supposed to go out on weekends," I say automatically, and then I stop when she frowns at me.

"What do you mean? Your aunt doesn't lock you up, does she?"

I cover my mouth, shaking my head. "No, no. I—" What do I say? "Let me make sure my aunt doesn't need me. She's sick."

Emily gives me a sympathetic look. "I heard. Clara Atherton's like a legend in this area. I think it's wonderful that you're here to help."

I want to say that my aunt is helping me. "Thank you for thinking of me," I say softly, shyly. I've never had a female friend before. It feels nice. Since Father doesn't let me go anywhere, most girls ignore me.

"Sure. I should tell you: Kenji swears he thinks you're the prettiest girl in school." At my look of terror, she stops. "Oh, don't worry. I'm not asking you to the movies so my brother can hit on you. He's gay. Actually, he's bi. Or experimenting." She shrugs. "Hard to say. He seems to enjoy people, how's that? Have you noticed, Dario's been hiding? Kenji told him that if he comes near us again, he'll lose the family jewels."

After class, Emily tells me she'll meet me in the cafeteria and jokes to "look for the big Japanese guy sitting at the table." I'm almost to math class when Rory appears and grabs me by the wrist. Before I can protest, he pushes me into the girls' restroom, locking the door so we're alone in there.

"Do you regret it? What you did to us? What you did to Blake?" he demands angrily, his hand tightening on my wrist.

I wince. "Every day," I admit.

That makes Rory angrier. He flings me into the wall, hard enough to hurt a little. "You're such a liar!" he roars at me. "Because of you, he was arrested for rape!"

I want to tell Rory the truth, but I know no one can protect me. Jin and I may be stronger together, but Father kept us apart to keep us weaker. He used us against each other. Who's to say that if I tell the truth now that Father – or Brett – wouldn't do something? And maybe something in me is broken. Maybe I don't have the strength to fight anymore.

I'll protect you from the dark, I promise, Ara. Nothing bad will happen.

If only I could go back in time… "Is he—" I break off. "How is Blake?"

Rory's face contorts in rage. He grabs me by the shoulders and slams me against the wall. My teeth slam together hard. "How's Blake?! Now you ask? Well, let's see, after the charges were dropped, people still whispered about him behind his back. He was seventeen, but they were going to try him as an adult!" Breathing heavily, he brings his face close to mine. "I used to think you were the most wonderful thing in the world. So delicate. Sweet."

Tears slip from my eyes. "I'm sorry."

But Rory doesn't hear me. "You still smell like peaches. Your skin…" His voice grows strangely hoarse. For a moment he looks away, breathing heavily. Then he turns back. He grabs my head and kisses me, his body pressing me against the wall. When he pulls back, the look he gives me is a cross between lust and horror.

"The world would be better without you," he says, refusing to look at me.

I flinch as he leaves, the door banging behind him. Gathering my things, I walk to class. When I enter, Rory doesn't look at me and I don't look at him. We both sit in silence.

Kenji stretches at the lunch table. He's not doing it to show off, but his broad shoulders ripple even under his uniform. To be honest, I'm surprised there's a uniform that fits him. If I think about it, he's attractive. But as soon as the thought enters my mind, I tamp it down in guilt. Old habits die hard.

"Are you going home for Thanksgiving or Christmas?" Kenji asks me, starting on his second sandwich. He eats a lot.

I shake my head. "No, I'll stay with my aunt."

"What about your twin brother?" Emily asks.

"Jin." My voice hitches a little and Emily notices the change in my voice. "I hope I'll see him soon."

"Why wouldn't your family fly your brother out? You two seem close." Kenji shoves the rest of his sandwich in his mouth.

I'm not sure what to say. If I tell them the truth, will they make fun of me? And if I lie, what kind of person does that make me? A liar, a monster. Rory's last words to me: *The world would be better without you.* It stings, but he's not wrong.

"My father thinks I'm a bad influence on Jin," I say finally.

Emily pauses with a French fry halfway to her mouth. "Excuse me?"

I shake my head. "I make Jin act out. He gets into trouble because of me." I find it hard to swallow my food. I take a sip of water.

Emily exchanges a look with her older brother. "Okay. So, a movie this weekend, maybe go shopping for a Halloween costume?"

"Costume?"

"For the party, silly," Emily says, bumping her shoulder with mine. She glances at the Idols' table. "I swear, Rory Remington stares at you a lot."

I glance over. Rory is looking right at me. Our eyes meet before he turns away to talk to Jaylen Strauss.

"The girls who hang out with the Idol boys frequently dress as sexy devils," Kenji says in a bored voice.

I agree that it doesn't sound very original.

"Anyway, everyone goes to the Halloween party!" Emily does this chipper clapping thing with her hands. "That's it, we're finding a costume and grabbing lunch this weekend!"

I open my mouth to protest, but Kenji wags his finger at me. "No, don't fight Emily on this. She's unstoppable when she's focused."

CHAPTER 8

At first, I think about telling Emily that I feel sick. But Jin tells me it would be rude. Eventually, he tells me that Father will never know. Ellen gives me an odd look when I ask for Aunt Clara's permission; it's no odder than the steely glare Aunt Clara gives me when I ask.

After going back on forth on what to wear – it's cooler now, so sweats are not unreasonable – I finally pick jeans and a long-sleeved blouse. It isn't too snug, and the blouse is long, covering my tummy and hiding my bottom. I'm starting to get used to the uniform, although I always feel half-naked with my legs exposed.

Emily makes Kenji sit in the back so I can sit in the front with her. He takes it with a good-natured grin. "I'm looking for costumes, too. I have thought about being Geralt from *The Witcher.*"

When I tell him I'm not familiar with the character, Kenji launches into a long description of the character and the tv series. Emily just tells me we're going to the coolest costume shop ever.

Emily explains that Cove Prep attracts a lot of very rich families. Rich families mean money spent on nonessential items. "Halloween is one of the few parties where you don't need a date," Emily explains as we go through the women's costumes. Kenji's disappeared off somewhere. "So…. Feel like telling me the history between you and Rory Remington? The real history? I honestly don't buy his story that you're an easy lay. You're the only one I know who hasn't modified her uniform to show off her body more."

I flush, pretending to look at a dress. "Do you know Blake Remington?" I finally ask.

Emily makes a humming sound. "Yes. Rumor has it that he was almost sent to jail for rape."

"I'll tell you the truth. But… during lunch. And if you don't want to be friends anymore, I'll understand," I tell her.

Emily cocks her head at me. "You're very serious for seventeen. Alright, over lunch." Her dark eyes grow wide. "Oh, my God. I found the perfect thing for you!"

Emily drags me to the back, showing me a dress that mimics the costumes used in a show called *The Empress of China*. It's a *hanfu* following the designs from the Tang Dynasty. It's red, decorated with pale pink flowers, and the matching *ruqun* hangs open over the shoulders like a cape.

"I know you're not Chinese, but this is you. You *need* this outfit! You've got the right coloring and height." Emily gushes about the dress. "Look, if you get this and wear it to the party, I promise to wear whatever you pick out for me. Even if it's a Big Bird costume."

After a few more minutes of wheedling, I finally agree, cursing my spineless personality. And then, I pick out a ninja costume for her because she reminds me of a fierce fighter. When Kenji finds us, he's picked out – you guessed it – a Geralt costume. He even plans on bleaching his hair. I try not to wince thinking about it.

The shop owner packages our costumes carefully and sends us off.

It's weird eating out in the open. I keep expecting someone to yell at me or scold me. But no one looks at me oddly. I fumble over ordering food, letting Emily and Kenji order first so I get an idea of how to do it.

"Alright, spill. You and Rory," Emily demands, snapping her fingers impatiently.

My eyes grow unfocused. "We were friends. Rory, Jin, and me. He was going on thirteen when we met. His family moved into a rental near us. It was for a year. I don't know all of the details, but there was some sort of land deal my father was involved in. Rory's father was involved, too. When we met in school, Rory, Jin, and I became fast friends. Blake and my older brother Brett hated each other. Blake was a junior then, Brett was a senior." I take a steadying breath. "The summer was my best summer ever. We had a lot of fun. Blake was not like Brett. Brett…" I run my finger along my water glass. "Brett is hard to get along with."

Both Emily and Kenji listen quietly. "What happened then?" Emily asks gently.

"My father threw a party one night in August. Rory, Jin, and I planned on playing games together. It was a treat. My father was – is – very strict. Back then, I was to be in bed at eight. Earlier in the day, I got my dress dirty. Father was upset so he put me in my room. I wasn't allowed to go to the party." I gloss over him beating me with a belt. I lick my lips. "No one told me what had happened. But he told the police I'd seen Blake leave the library." I hunch my shoulders. "I didn't see Blake leave the library."

"But that would be lying," I tell Father. "I thought we weren't supposed to lie. I saw Brett—"

Father never hits me in the face. It's too easy for the world to see if there are marks on your face. So, when he slaps me across the cheek, I know he's serious. But I resist. He threatens to take Jin away. And when I keep insisting that I saw Brett, not Blake, he removes his belt and beats me until my skin breaks. Then, to make the pain stop, to see Jin again, I agree.

"I didn't know that a girl had been assaulted. But I – wanted to please my father." I look at my hands. They're shaking. "The girl…" Marigold Summers.

Brett was fascinated by her hair. "She didn't see who hurt her." Marigold had been a little drunk. He'd put a blanket over her face. "I think it was too much for her. She changed her story. Said nothing happened, it was consensual."

I have nightmares about Marigold. The justice she never got. Because of me.

"You were just a kid. I could be wrong, but your dad seems a little controlling," Emily says bluntly. Kenji nods gently in agreement.

"It's just how he is," I whisper. "So, Rory has a good reason to hate me. And I deserve it. And I understand if this changes how you view me."

Kenji crosses his huge arms. The food arrives and he waits as his two burgers are placed in front of him. When the server leaves, he says, "Nothing has changed for me. You should know you can come to me if you feel you are not safe."

I lower my head, hiding the tears in my eyes. Kindness. Something I don't deserve. And yet… I won't reject it. Not now when I feel so lost without Jin.

"I agree. You were a kid and you didn't know anything." Emily huffs. "Guys are so judgmental." She winks at her brother. "Well, I don't care about being popular so you can hang with me any time you want. Sometimes having a big older brother is nice."

I think sourly of Brett. *Not always,* I think.

I'm in bed shivering. I lied. I don't know what's going on, but I need to tell Rory that Father made me lie. My body aches, but I've dealt with pain before. I make a decision.

Easing open my window, I look out. From here, I can see the lights on at the Remingtons. Maybe if I tell them how Father is like sometimes, they'll understand and help me. Rory will protect me because he said so.

Slowly, I step out on the ledge. From there, I just need to walk over to Rory's room and climb down the trellis. Out of nowhere, I hand snakes out. I give a little gasp when Brett holds me outside my window by the waist.

"Hello, little sister. What are you doing outside?"

Why is Brett in my room? He has me pinned to his chest. I'm close to his face, and I can smell the alcohol. "Brett, you scared me." I glance over my shoulder at him. "Could you – could you please bring me inside?"

"It seems like you were going somewhere, Laura. Where were you going? Father is going to be so disappointed when I tell him."

"Please. Please don't tell him. Please, I was just…" I can't think of anything.

Brett shifts suddenly and I squeal when he maneuvers me so that he's holding me out the window by my wrists.

My feet scramble for purchase but find none. "Brett. Please. Please, don't let go."

"You think I'd kill my little sister? What kind of monster do you think I am?" Brett smiles at me as I crane my neck to look at him. For a moment, I believe

him. "From this height, you won't die."

And then he lets go. I'm so shocked that I barely have time to scream as pain rips through me.

CHAPTER 9

The school rents a building for the annual Halloween party. I meet Emily at her home, and we get ready together. It's weird, and I find myself smiling with excitement. Emily's family lives in this beautiful mansion by a lake that has swans in it – although it's late in the season so the swans have left.

Emily is positively dangerous looking as a ninja. With her athletic body, she could be a character from G.I. Joe. As promised, Kenji had a salon bleach his hair and now he is Geralt. With his physique, he certainly could play the part.

Emily helps me put my hair into a bun – she's a lot better than I am doing hair – and throws enough molding wax into my hair to keep it in place. I feel like a walking fire hazard.

She helps me into my costume and after we get everything secured and tied, I stare at my reflection in dismay.

"What's wrong?" Emily asks. "The fit is fabulous!"

The red color suits my skin. The silk moves around me like a dream, but I'm staring at my cleavage. Tears come to my eyes. "Too much of my skin is exposed," I say, my breathing a little rapid.

"It looks fine. It doesn't look slutty," Emily assures me, but I shake my head, tears spilling.

"No. No, if my father sees me like this, he'll –" I break off, shoving a hand to my mouth.

Emily grabs some tissues and forces me to sit. "I don't know what's going on with your father, Laura, but your father is not going to be at this party. He will never see you. He won't hear about it."

"I can't stay out too late." I let Emily blot my face.

"Just tell us when you're tired." She keeps wiping until the tears stop. "Laura, if you're in danger from your father—"

"I'm not," I interrupt her. "I'm sorry. I didn't mean to be rude."

Emily sighs. "How about I do a little makeup?"

I flinch. "I'm not supposed to wear makeup." Why can't I shut up?

Emily ignores me, dusting my face with powder. "Luckily, you were blessed with some nice features." She runs lipstick over my lips. "There. Simple. Okay?"

By the time we're in the car, I feel calmer. Kenji drives us to the party.

Even though it's six, the world is dark. I think it's too early for snow, but I'm not sure. I've never been on the East Coast before.

Going through the gates, the experience is surreal. I've never been out after dark since I was twelve. After that summer, Father became stricter. I stare at the students, some very scantily clad, others in outrageous getups. I see everything from zombies to Teenage Mutant Ninja Turtles. I want to clap like I'm twelve again.

Kenji helps me and his sister out, extending a huge arm to each of us as we make our way into the building. Everything is a visual delight: the chandeliers, the lights, the decorations. At every turn, there is another costume to admire. Is this what teenagers do? Some of the guys are jostling each other in good humor. Girls primp as they take pictures.

"Are you into booze? There's a booze table over there," Emily says, pointing to a corner.

I shake my head, and Kenji says, "I'm more of a soda fan myself."

We find another table with more innocuous beverages. I'm not quite sure what to grab.

"The lemonade is good," the boy next to me suggests.

My eyes grow wide when I realize Zyair Campos is talking to me. All the Idol boys are fairly attractive, and Zyair is no exception. He slowly looks at me from head to toe. I instinctively cross my arms to cover my exposed skin.

"Now *that* is a costume," he says approvingly. "You look like an Asian empress. Or concubine."

He's dressed as Zorro and the costume suits his deeply tanned skin. I try not to cringe at his words. Emily sees me hunching and sighs. "Come on, Laura, put your hands down. It's not like your boobs are falling out."

"Please do," Zyair drawls. "You have pretty skin."

I do a quick one-eighty. I feel dirty – I remember how angry Father got when my body developed. Kenji quickly comes to the rescue. "Zyair, please try to be polite. It is rude to ogle girls like that. She is a person, not an object."

Even though Kenji is not an Idol, people try not to make Kenji upset. Zyair shrugs. "She looks hot. Nothing wrong with telling a girl she looks hot." Zyair looks behind me. "What do you think, Rory? I'm thinking she's too gorgeous to pass up."

"Go fuck yourself, Zyair," Rory snaps. He's dressed as Prince Charming. How… ironic. He grabs my arm. "I need to talk to you. Now."

Emily gets huffy and Kenji is ready to intervene. I wave them off. "It's okay."

Rory keeps holding my arm until we find a quiet spot in one of the hallways. "The other day. When I said the world would be a better place without you. I didn't mean that I wanted you dead." He then looks at my outfit. "You do look… really nice."

"Thank you." My voice is barely a whisper.

"I'm not saying I care what happens to you," Rory continues. "I don't want you crying to people. Knowing you, you'd pretend to hurt yourself and then have authorities come after me."

I keep my arms crossed over my chest, my eyes on the floor. Very slowly, his hands come up and move my hands and arms to the side. I turn bright red. I feel horribly exposed.

"I know we were just kids, but I used to think you liked me. When we hung out. You, me, Jin." His breathing is uneven as he continues to stare at me. "I had all these feelings that confused the shit out of me. I was going to beg Dad to find a way to stay so I could be close to you. Of course, now that I know what kind of person you are… I guess I got lucky."

Involuntarily, he runs a finger along a clavicle. I tense, but I don't move. "Do your new friends know what kind of liar you are? How you'll do anything so your father can win? You're lucky I don't tell people the details about you. It's only to protect Blake." He leans his head forward. "If I see you with Kenji, I'll expose you. And it won't be just the girls after you. I'll send everyone after you."

A single tear runs down my cheek. He wipes it with a finger.

"Don't cry, Ara," he sneers, using my nickname hatefully. "I'm sure you'll find a way to fool someone. But not at my school. I rule here. I see you using your face to lure another guy and you will learn what it's like to be bullied and tortured."

Bullied and tortured? I laugh. I can't help myself, and it shocks me as much as it shocks him. I just laugh, and it sounds borderline hysterical. I keep laughing even when he shakes me.

"Stop it."

I can't. I laugh harder. Tortured? He doesn't know the meaning of the word. I'm hysterical as he shakes me harder. His blue eyes grow wide with fury. When my laughter pauses as I struggle to suck in air, he kisses me again to shut me up.

"What the hell are you doing, Rory?!" Paris Dumonte screeches, storming over in her princess dress.

Rory throws me back as Paris walks over to us. "She threw herself at me again, what do you think?"

If I had the wherewithal to laugh again, I would. Instead, I stand there like a mute moron. Paris raises her hand to hit me, and Rory swiftly blocks her.

"What are you doing, Paris? I don't belong to you," he says in a cruel voice.

I use that opportunity to make my escape. I ignore Rory calling my name sharply, and Paris screeching at Rory about me.

And then, because I'm cursed, I run into Jaylen Strauss. "Whoa!" The funny part? He's dressed like a cowboy. His surprise is evident when he sees me. "You look like you're not having a very good time," he observes. "Which is a shame because you're clearly wearing the best costume here."

I don't even know how he manages to do this, but he guides me on to the dance floor. "I don't dance," I whisper, the color fleeing my face.

"It'd be a shame to be wearing something so sumptuous and not take it for a spin on the dance floor," Jaylen continues, oblivious to my distress.

I'm not sure what I'm doing, but, somehow, I manage to follow his lead. I figure the long folds of the *hanfu* hide my awkward movements. I feel like everyone is staring at us. Emily smiles from the corner. Kenji seems to be flirting with someone dressed as a Klingon, but even he stops to give me a nod of approval. And then Rory shows up with Paris clinging to his arm again. In the light, his black hair gleams as he glares at us with a mixture of anger and something else.

"Ah, there he is," Jaylen observes, "the guy who says you're nothing to him. And yet he can't keep his eyes off you. Not that I blame him. You're easy on the eyes even if you look terrified half the time."

My brows rise in surprise.

"You certainly don't speak very much," Jaylen says in that same easygoing manner. "You aren't what I expected you to be, that's for sure. Rory painted a she-devil. But for some reason, I think you're like a bird in a cage." When I remain silent, he adds, "A quiet bird." The song ends and he releases me. "Now shoo before Rory hits me."

I don't need to be told twice. For the rest of the night, Emily and Kenji shield me. I watch Rory dance with Paris all night long. I don't need to be told that I'm nothing. I already know it.

It's February. Jin had to stay home today because he was sick. This is the first time since Rory started at our school that we've been alone together. It's a dreary day. The clouds made the sun so dim that it feels like seven p.m., not three.

"Do you like being here?" I ask, a little breathless with the brisk walk.

Rory stops to adjust the hat on my head, his blue eyes shining down at me. "I do."

"It's a shame you're only here until the end of the year," I say shyly. "Jin doesn't always make friends easily."

We stop walking for a minute. "I want to ask you something," Rory says, the color high in his face.

Snow starts to fall around us. I look up and laugh a little. "What do you want to ask?"

"I think I want you to be my first kiss," he says, pretending to ignore my surprise.

"What?"

Rory puffs himself up. "Just a peck. On the lips. That way, we'll always have that memory even after we move away."

To my twelve-year-old brain, it makes sense, but I'm worried about Father. "You won't tell anyone, will you? Father wouldn't approve."

Rory tilts his head. "You sure care a lot about what your dad thinks. But no, I won't tell anyone."

I give him a tiny smile and lean forward, closing my eyes. The kiss is short, sweet, chaste. More of a peck. But when we straighten, Rory has this secret smile of satisfaction on his face that I don't understand. I let him hold my hand until we get within a block of home. I don't want anyone to see us being so close.

CHAPTER 10

I don't need Ellen to tell me that Aunt Clara is not doing well. I think she's gotten used to me. I visit her almost every day, reading quietly or sometimes just telling her about what I'm learning in school.

Jin is wracking his brains about making his way out to the East Coast to visit me. We're worried Father will find out and will find a way to stop us. We don't want a reason for him to track us down. Although Mother's relatives are nice to him, they're clueless about why Jin never gets to come home.

The longer Jin is away, the more broken I feel. In our talks, I think we both feel the strain. Sometimes I cry myself to sleep. I'd managed to gain some weight during September and October, but I'm struggling as Thanksgiving approaches.

The girls haven't let up. I've learned to avoid the restrooms unless necessary. Rory rarely is directly involved, but when things are thrown at me or shoved my way, I frequently see him smirking.

"I'm just saying you should try out for the talent show or maybe the play we're doing next semester," Emily suggests. We're walking to the parking lot together to head home.

"I don't know. I don't really have any—" I break off in horror as Emily curses.

Someone has scratched the word 'bitch' into the hood of the Range Rover. It's not my Range Rover. It's Aunt Clara's. Her property. It's damaged. Oh, God.

"What is this scratch on the car, Laura? I don't remember seeing it this morning."

No. No. What if she tells Father? How will I pay for the repairs?

Emily examines the hood. "I think you'll need a new paint job."

I'm stricken with terror. I glance around the parking lot and find Rory and Paris watching in delight. Emily follows my gaze.

"Those assholes!" She starts to storm over.

I collapse to the ground. No. No. I don't want to go back.

"I told you, Laura, to treat my things with respect."

"It wasn't me. I swear, it wasn't me." I start crying.

"It's either you or Jin!"

My throat closes. I don't know what to do.

"Brett, hold her down. She'll tell me the truth when I'm done with her."

Aunt Clara will be furious. She'll send me back. Father will be angry. More than angry. I can't breathe. He will… Brett will help him. I don't want them to touch me. My hands clench against the asphalt, the gravel digging into my skin. Can't breathe. I claw at my throat. I can't go back. I can't go back now that I know what it's like to wake up.

"Hey, Laura, it's no biggie. Kenji probably knows someone." Emily is back beside me, but I can't see her.

"I don't want to go back," I whimper.

"What? Laura, talk to me. The hood can be fixed."

I stand up. I think someone grabs my arm, but I shake it off. I have to run. I can't go home. Here, Father couldn't find me. I could run now. I don't have to go back. Brett and Father can't find me. My hands go to my hair and I pull. I pull until the pain snaps me into action. I run.

I run and keep running. Buildings, hallways, steps, doors. I can run faster than Brett. I know I can.

"Please, please don't send me back!" I scream.

"You can see, she's distraught. She's attacked her older brother," Father tells the staff. *"I'm worried about my family's safety."*

I see the doors. If I can reach the doors, I'll be free. I run. "Don't send me back! I'll do anything!"

The hands. I have to escape the hands that hold me.

I won't go back. I close my eyes. I can feel the breeze. I'm close. I just need to step out the doors into the cold, crisp breeze. The promise of freedom.

"Ara, what are you doing?"

My eyes open. I'm high up. I could fly. Fly away from the monsters. Then Jin will be free. He can run, too. The weakest link. I'm the weakest link.

"Ara, look at me. It's Rory. Turn around and look at me."

"Laura, please get away from the ledge. Come on, we can fix this." Emily.

"I don't want to go back. Please don't lock me up. I promise. I promise I'll be good. I won't say anything." I pull at my hair. "It's always my fault. Always."

"Laura, God, you're bleeding!"

"Ara, please look at me. What are you doing? Jin needs you, right?"

I freeze. Slowly, I look over my shoulder. This can't be right. Rory is never there when Father locks me up.

"I've got money," Emily says, and I think she's weeping. "I can fix the car. No one needs to know."

I'm confused. "I can't go back."

Rory takes a step closer, his hand extended. "Come on, Ara, take my hand. Come to me, okay? Jin's waiting."

I stare down at my hands. They're covered in hair and blood. My hair. My blood.

"Tell Blake I'm sorry," I whisper, leaning.

Emily screams.

Rory is faster. He grabs me before I can fall. We fall back onto the ground.

I stare into his blue eyes in shock. "Why did you do that?" I ask brokenly before weeping uncontrollably.

"Thank you for bringing her home," Ellen says briskly. "She'll get medical attention immediately."

Rory raises his voice. "She needs to see a doctor! She ripped out chunks of her hair and tried to jump off a building!"

"Please lower your voice, young man," Ellen continues. "Who damaged the car?"

Rory pauses. "Several girls from the school. They're – jealous of her."

"Ms. Atherton is not well enough for visitors. I will make sure her niece is taken care of and we will contact the school to talk about the bullying."

"I want to talk to Laura again."

"No, the nurse is with her. I must ask you to leave."

"Does her aunt know the meaning behind her words?! Because it made no fucking sense to me!"

"Laura is sedated. Ms. Atherton is aware of Laura's health and has taken great pains to help her. Unfortunately, something triggered this setback." Ellen's voice is hard. "If you happen to know who triggered it, then you may stay and explain. Otherwise, leave before I call the police."

A few minutes later, Ellen comes in. The nurse gives me some pain pills and I swallow them. Ellen brushes my hair back. "Well, luckily you have a lot of hair. It doesn't look too bad. I want you to take a nap, okay? Don't worry about the car. Don't worry about anything."

"I'm sorry," I whimper. "Don't let Father know."

"Just get some rest."

They turn off the light and leave me in the dark.

CHAPTER 11

After Thanksgiving, the Range Rover shows up with a new paint job. Emily says it wasn't her. I stare at it from the window. When I talk to Jin, I tell him about my episode. He tells me it's normal. He tells me it's PTSD and that there's nothing wrong with me, but I'm not sure. Ellen assures me that Aunt Clara would never call Father about anything so minor as a scratch on a car.

Returning to school after Thanksgiving break, I'm self-conscious. With a new cut, you can't really tell that I yanked some of my hair out. Ellen has my hair pulled back in a scarf to hide the patches that are still healing. But even though Emily says that there weren't a lot of students who saw me panicking, I feel like everyone's staring.

Rory corners me before my first class with Emily. "I've been trying to reach you," he says, his blue eyes on my face. "I think we need to talk. We need to have a serious talk." He lowers his voice. "Ara, have you tried to hurt yourself before?"

I flinch when his hand rises. A flash of pain and the hand falls. I push him away. "There's nothing wrong with me!" I spit out defensively.

Students stare at us as I gape in horror. I can't believe I raised my voice like that. I cover my mouth. I quickly walk into class, but I'm completely on edge. Emily's there, her smile telling me she's there for me. Her acceptance, her ability not to judge me, gnaws at me. I promise to explain things to her – but she's not daft. She understands a lot more than she lets on. She tells me that Kenji will walk me from lunch to my next class to minimize the girls coming after me.

It's not until math class that I face Rory again. It would be more accurate to say that I face him on my way to math class, but I ignore him.

"I am not leaving you alone until you promise to talk to me," he whispers behind me.

"I thought you said the world would be better without me," I say dully.

Rory sucks in his breath. "You know I didn't mean it."

We can't speak further because class begins, but Rory won't let up. He follows me after math class to the lunchroom, blocking me from entering. He grabs my arm.

"Don't," I whisper, losing all color.

He drops his hand again, and this time he lets the pain show. "Laura, I won't hurt you."

I think about when he pushed me against my car and when he cornered me in the restroom. He's more than capable of hurting me. That's not why I'm flinching. I can't let him get too close. Some of my thoughts must show on my face because guilt shines clearly through his eyes. "I'm sorry about my behavior when I first saw you. I won't..." His voice trails off as he fights for control. "I'm worried about you."

"I'm fine." My gaze slides away. "Rory..."

Without warning, he grabs me, firmly but gently, and clasps me to his chest like I'm something precious. His heart pounds loudly in my ear. "Please talk to me. Laura, what happened on the roof... What's going on?"

I can't tell him anything. He'll confront Father. And then he'll learn things about me that I don't want him to know.

"This weekend. Can we talk this weekend? Just you and me." He's begging and pleading, and it makes my heart hurt. "You talk, I'll listen. I promise I won't yell. I—Trust me this one time."

He tucks a strand of hair that escaped the scarf behind my ear. I want to say yes.

"Rory, what is going on?"

Paris glares at us, but Rory doesn't pull away. "Mind your own business, Paris. And stay the fuck away from Laura."

Paris shrieks. "You told me to go after her."

"I've changed my mind. Now get the fuck away from us before you make me truly angry!"

She shrieks a curse before leaving.

I'm trembling. "I'll talk to you this weekend," I say numbly. What am I doing? I don't know anymore.

"I—I'm trying to sort this out, Ara. But I'm not walking away until I know the truth."

My face is grim. "Sometimes the truth is worse than the lie."

"I'm afraid this isn't the first time she's tried to kill herself," I hear Father tell the doctor. I'm heavily sedated. My leg is broken from Brett dropping me. The bruises on my back supposedly came from my fall.

"We'll admit her. She's young and prone to hysteria," someone says to my father.

I want to tell them no. I have to tell Rory the truth.

"I'm worried about my family's safety," Father says in a worried voice. "How long can you keep her?"

"I'd like to keep her sedated for a week so her leg can heal a bit. Perhaps a few weeks while we try different medications."

I'm not sick. I didn't try to kill myself. Please don't do this. Why won't any-

one hear me? Why won't anyone listen?

Brett comes in. "I'd like to say goodbye to my sister. Privately."

He sits on the bed and peers into my face. I blink at him slowly. I can't find the energy to speak. He leans so that his mouth is by my ear.

"I know what you were going to do. You were going to tell that Rory kid the truth. Let me tell you how things are going to go. We're going to leave you here until your brain turns to mush. You try to reach out to Rory or anyone in his family, and I will kill you. Before I kill you, I will do very horrible things to your body so that when Jin sees you, he'll cry. He'll cry like the dumb baby he is. I want you to think very carefully about what you do when we bring you home." He straightens up and gives me a sweet smile. "I'm going to miss you, squirt. You get better and come home."

When Brett leaves, I want to scream. But no sound comes out. And even if it did, would anyone listen?

The weekend looms like a harbinger of doom. I'm not sure how much I can (or am willing) to tell Rory. There's a risk. A risk to me. A risk to Jin. A risk even to Rory that he wouldn't understand. There are days when I'm not sure what's even real anymore.

It's easy to hide and let bygones be bygones. I think of Marigold Summers. She was the age that I am now, at a party where the adults didn't notice she was drinking or didn't care. No one noticed when she disappeared.

After I learned the truth, the grief and guilt got hard to bear. I imagined her pain and suffering and my complicit contribution to that pain. It got to be too much. Rory might hate me, but I hate myself, too.

When I got better, Jin and I would lie in bed, dreaming. We'd move to a small town. He'd find work, and I would wait tables. We'd save and go to college online. I would find Marigold Summers. Finding her in person would be too risky. Brett might find us. Instead, I'd write a letter to her and Blake. We'd drive out to the middle of nowhere to mail it and then settle in a small town – a town where everyone notices an outsider. We'd become part of the community. If Brett or Father ever found us, the town would alert us.

Sometimes we'd embellish the details. Jin would buy me a dress. I would go to a party and stay out after ten. Jin would have a drink and meet a nice girl. I would accept flowers from someone without repercussions. We'd eat a lot and get fat and happy. We wouldn't wash the dishes right away. We wouldn't lock our bedroom doors at night out of fear.

I've read enough books for school, seen enough things at school, to know that the life Jin and I lead is not normal. But no one's looked close enough to notice. You see, no one looks too hard at the quiet ones.

CHAPTER 12

Aunt Clara is getting worse. I see the pain and discomfort in her face, and now I'm riddled with fear. On Saturday morning, I drop by, but she tells me not to read. Instead, we sit in companionable silence. The nurse and Ellen hover in the background.

"I don't think I'll make it to June," she says softly, not looking at me. She's gazing at something I can't see. "I'm trying to set something up for you."

"You'll make it," I say earnestly. "My favorite season is spring even if the flowers make me sneeze." I'm babbling, but I don't know what else to say. I take her very weak hand in mine. "Please don't leave me, Clara."

"I want you to go out with that Remington boy today. Don't think I don't know what's going on in your life," she rasps out with dry humor.

"I can stay here," I offer, but she shakes her head.

"No. No, I'm too tired. Come back later. Tell me later." My aunt closes her eyes. "I thought I had more time."

Ellen helps me out when I start crying. "You need to be strong for her," she tells me sternly, but not without sympathy. Ellen is not unaffected. There is a rough friendship between her and my aunt. "Whatever happens, you don't go back into that hole. You fight. You become a fighter like your aunt. Do you think you can do that?"

Fight. The last time I tried, I ended up in the hospital. I stopped fighting because it made things easier. Now that I've been away from Father and Brett, I know that I'd rather die than go back there. Which means I fight.

I'm solemn by the time Rory picks me up. I wear a dark blue dress with tights. It has long sleeves, and the hemline is right at the knees. I don't think it's too flashy, but I've gotten used to the skirts for the uniforms, so it doesn't feel too risqué.

Even though I have a nice wool coat with me, Rory has the car nice and toasty. He glances at me periodically during the drive – to be honest, I'm not sure where we're going – but he doesn't engage me in conversation.

Finally, I break the silence. "Aunt Clara isn't doing well. I don't want to be gone too long."

I don't understand the expression on his face – maybe disappointment? – but it clears. "Of course. I thought I'd take you to lunch."

I frown. This isn't a date, right? And why am I asking myself that? I try to keep my hands idle on my lap. Why am I in a car with a boy who wanted to hurt me? And did he?

Rory's blue eyes look at me when we're paused at a stoplight. "You look nice," he says a bit awkwardly.

Am I supposed to say the same? I don't know. I return his look blankly. Maybe I look scared because his jaw tenses. He's unhappy.

You know how I hate to be displeased.

I flinch as my father's words enter my mind. I quickly avert my gaze and stare out the window. We arrive at a small seaside building that looks like a lodge. There's a man who opens my door, and Rory hands him the keys and cash before placing a hand at my back. I flinch again and he drops the hand.

Rory is a striking individual, so it doesn't surprise me that several people stare at him openly. Rory glowers.

"Ah, Mr. Remington. Your table is ready," a uniformed man says to him, leading us to a dining alcove where there is one table set for two.

Okay, so Rory wants a very private conversation. Rory does this weird thing where he makes sure I'm seated before sitting down himself. We order our beverages – iced tea for me, lemonade for Rory – and then Rory tells them to just bring the food when ready. He then gestures the server to leave.

"Assholes in the lobby," he mutters as soon as we're alone.

"What?"

"The guys in the lobby. Checking you out. You're fucking seventeen. They need to keep their damn eyes to themselves." Rory looks furious.

"Are you sure they were looking at us?"

"There's the possibility one or two of them is gay, but I'm pretty sure they were looking at you." He stretches his neck and makes an effort to calm down. "Your aunt is not well? I'm sorry to hear that. I don't know the specifics of her illness, but I presume cancer?"

I nod.

"You know, I didn't even think about the similar last names," he muses out loud. "Clara Atherton's been in this area forever. When we moved here a few years back, she'd already become reclusive. She took back her maiden name after her husband's death, right?"

"Yes."

His eyes become veiled. "I suppose you stand to gain when she dies. Are you her designated heir?"

Oh, that's a loaded question. "I don't know," I answer honestly. My father is many things, including greedy. In my darkest thoughts, I've wondered what would he do to me to get the rest of the money? It's one of the reasons why Jin and I don't plan to hang around.

"I don't want the money," I finally say, because that is the truth. I add bitterly, "My father can have it all."

"Your father. You lied for him, yet you sound like you hate him." There's a challenge in his words.

"I do hate him." I surprise myself with my honesty. Where did that come from? I grow silent when the server comes in with salads and four different kinds of pasta.

After food is plated for me, Rory tells the man, "Don't come back until I ring the bell."

I quirk a brow at him, but he just shrugs, gesturing for me to continue. "It all changed that night, didn't it? Our friendship. Our lives. I think about it… a lot," I admit.

"Your father got the contract, you know. Not that it mattered." He picks up a cherry tomato and eats it. "My mother inherited a significant amount of money over three years ago. With that, my father's business has grown. So, in the long run, the contract was nothing."

"I didn't go to the party." Rory frowns at my words.

"I know. You were sick."

"I wasn't sick." I take a deep breath. "I'm taking a risk telling you some of this, so you need to promise me something. I don't even know why I'm telling you. Maybe I'm tired. Maybe I'm breaking." Maybe I'm going crazy? "But you need to make a promise to me first."

"Tell me and I'll decide if it's worthy."

"No. No, Rory, I need you to make me a promise with no conditions. If you want to know what happened, you have to promise, and you're not allowed to ask why." I cross my arms stubbornly.

Rory's blue eyes stare at me for a long time. "What's the promise?"

"You can't confront my father. Or Brett. At least, not right away." I don't clue him in on my potential escape when I'm eighteen. I twist my hands in my lap. He can do whatever he wants when I'm gone.

Mouth tense, Rory considers this, his nostrils flaring. "Fine. I promise."

Do I believe him? "I wore my dress for the party too soon. It got smudged with dirt because I was careless. Father was so angry that he sent me to my room."

"For a dirty dress?"

"I should have known better. I was old enough to stay clean. I was old enough to know not to wear my dress too soon. It's because girls are prone to vanity, which is why discipline is necessary." My words are mechanical. I can recite every reason at the top of my head. I blink and something akin to horror crosses Rory's face. "He wouldn't let Jin see me after…after my punishment. Father does that a lot. If I misbehave, he keeps us separated so that Jin can't comfort me. It's to keep our rebelliousness in check." I try to lift my glass but my hand trembles, so I leave it alone. Rory's face grows white.

"After the party, he started… He told me what to say about Blake. I didn't realize something had happened to Marigold, and I didn't understand why he wanted me to lie." I can't bring myself to look at Rory as I continue. "It's wrong to lie. I held out, you know. I didn't give in right away. But I got so tired. So hungry. I was sore. He never let me heal before he started again."

"What are you saying?" His voice shakes.

I sigh. "He made me repeat it until I had it perfect. Every time I made a mistake, he would –." I break off. "I made so many mistakes."

Rory suddenly swears. "Ara, your father beat you?" He rises to his feet, and I look at him in surprise. His body vibrates with rage. "He – hurt you? How long has this been going on?"

I don't say anything, but a single tear slips from my eye when I look away. After a moment, I manage to say, "You don't want to know what he does."

Rory makes a sound in his throat. "Ara, how long?" His eyes are filled with pain as he pieces my life together.

I shake my head as a few more tears escape. "You shouldn't ask that question, Rory."

"Tell me!"

My eyes flash with fury. "Why? You want to know if the paddle or belt hurts more? You want to know how often? Would that satisfy your curiosity?"

Rory moves around the table, grabbing me by the arms. "Did you lie because he hit you?"

Rory isn't listening. "I gave in because, after five days, I couldn't take it anymore. Because I was weak."

"No," he croaks, his hands running up and down my arms as if he's checking me for injuries.

I pull away. "You shouldn't touch me. Don't." His hands drop away.

"Ara, for God's sake, how long has thing been going on?" he demands hoarsely. "Ara, does your father do anything else to you? He doesn't… Does he touch you?"

I blink at him. "No, not that way." My arms press against my stomach. "There are rules I have to follow. No skirts. No jeans. Nothing tight. No bright colors. I'm not allowed to go out after six." I gesture to my dress. "I haven't worn a dress since that summer. It's weird."

The pallor leaves his face, replaced by darkening anger. "Laura, you know that isn't normal, right?"

I laugh bitterly. "Obviously. I'm not daft, Rory. The restrictions started after that night. I think partially to protect me from Brett."

"Your *brother?*"

"That's who I saw leaving the library," I whisper. "And when Brett saw me…" I remember thinking I would die. My hand goes to my throat. "He likes to watch when Father…" I can't finish the sentence. "After he disciplined me, Brett told Father."

Rory swears again, running a hand through his dark hair. "Your brother disciplined you? You make it sound like it's happened before. Ara." He pulls me into his arms, embracing me so tightly that I can't struggle free. "Don't pull away. For God's sake, let me hold you. I need to. I won't hurt you."

"I deserve it, you know. I'm weak. I've always been weak. I gave in, so I know why you hate me." My voice is slightly muffled because I'm pressed into his chest. "I won't fight back. I can take it. I just – I don't want Father to know."

Rory's whole body thrums with untold violence. "I'll kill them! I'll kill them for hurting you!" His touch is gentle against my head. "You should have told me this when I first saw you. Why didn't you? I shouldn't have treated you that way. It was just –." He breaks off.

I should pull away. Father would be disappointed in me. But I stay in his arms for a moment longer. "I hate myself, too, that's why."

"No, don't say that." He lifts my chin. "Shit, Laura, on that roof... I thought I was about to lose you and --." He stops, shaking his head. "The thought of losing you scared me. I've never felt like that before. But you've always affected me. You don't know how weird it is to have such intense feelings for someone when you're thirteen. To see you again after all this time... God, I messed up. I made it worse, didn't I? I let Dario grope you. I let Paris hurt you." He cups my face. "I'm so sorry. But it stops now. I won't hurt you. Never again. I won't let anyone else hurt you."

"There are some things you can't stop, Rory." But he ignores me, pressing feather-light kisses to my head. It feels good. After a brief hesitation, I tilt my head to give him better access to my neck, and he makes a deep sound of pleasure.

"You want me, too," he breathes, and this time he settles his mouth over mine. I don't answer him with words.

CHAPTER 13

I wake Sunday to a commotion. My head is still spinning from my day with Rory and how it ended. My lips still feel the tingle of his kisses. He didn't take it further, treating me gently and carefully like I'm fragile, but when he dropped me off, he promised me that things would be different Monday.

I rush downstairs when I hear Ellen yell. "Ellen, what's –?" I never finish my question.

My whole body freezes. Ellen and my father stand toe to toe. Brett walks right up to me, grabbing my chin. "Hello, little sister," he leers, enjoying how wide my eyes are.

I pinch myself. This is a dream. This is a nightmare.

"You cannot be here. Clara is not prepared for visitors," Ellen insists.

"This is my daughter. Clara is my sister. You think any police officer would let you throw me out?" he asks. "I'll have your bony-ass locked up!"

Ellen stutters, glancing at me. I give a faint shake of my head. My father suddenly sees me clearly, and his face darkens.

"What are you wearing?" he demands angrily.

I look down. I'm wearing jeans and a shirt. I bite my lip.

"Brett, take your sister to her room while I deal with this woman."

Ellen exchanges a helpless look with me. I want to tell her, *Don't fight. It only makes him angrier.* Likewise, I walk quietly to my room. There's no reason to incite Brett or my father.

Once there, I warily watch Brett close the door. "Change your clothes," he orders, his eyes sharp and predatory. There's always been something feral about Brett.

Wordlessly, I go to my closet and pull out some sweats and a baggy hoodie. I'm about to head to the bathroom when Brett blocks me.

"No, change here," he orders. "I want to be sure you don't do anything sneaky."

"Why are you here?" I ask, trying to buy time.

"We got a lovely call from your school. Or Father did." Terror rises when Brett smiles. "Sounds like someone reported that you tried to jump off a roof. You do have a habit of trying to kill yourself. We're just so worried about you. We rushed over right away."

No. No. No. I feel my world collapse and shrink.

"Now. Get changed."

I shake my head. "I'll do it in the bathroom."

Brett's fast. He's strong, too. Before I can run, he grabs me by the hair and slams my face down into the bed. I fight and scream, but he keeps my head pinned, my nose and mouth sealed by the bed as he straddles me from behind.

When my struggles weaken, he flips me over and begins to unbutton my jeans. I'm gasping as I make uncoordinated attempts to stop him. "Have you been whoring yourself out while you've been here?" he asks, hitting me in the stomach as he slips my jeans off. He holds me down with his body, clearly enjoying himself. "Letting boys touch you. Do all sorts of sinful things?"

I shake my head. I won't cry. I won't give him the satisfaction. I tense when Brett tightens a hand around my throat but then thinks better of it. He lets me go, throwing my sweats at me.

I get them on as quickly as I can, pulling the hoodie on. I'm covered. Modest. Shapeless. My older brother watches me like I'm prey, waiting for something. "What a nice room you have," he continues conversationally. "An upgrade. You've been living it up, haven't you?"

I put as much distance as I can between us, watching him as he continues to talk like we're friends. We stay that way for nearly thirty minutes until my father arrives.

"You'll be happy to know that I'm taking over my sister's care, Laura," Father says, smiling happily. "I'm sure you've missed your family. Mother will be here soon." He rubs his hands together. "Now, I understand you've been having some trouble adjusting."

"It was a mistake, an accident. Nothing happened," I blurt and then close my eyes.

"You've forgotten your manners." Father's face stiffens. "Brett, your sister has forgotten herself, has she not?"

"Oh, absolutely," Brett agrees. "She fought me on everything. She told me she wanted to dress like a slut."

I bite my tongue as Father sighs in disapproval. He starts to undo his belt. "Let me tell you how this is going to go, Laura. You will go to school tomorrow. And then you will come straight home. We'll see if we can fix your aunt's bad influence. Do you understand, Laura?"

My voice only trembles a little. I can't think too far ahead. "Yes, Father."

"Alright. Brett, hold her down in position for me," my father says, "I want to be sure to mete a proper punishment for her defiance."

CHAPTER 14

It's hard not to cry out at every bump in the road. But I'm tougher than I look. I grit my teeth. I don't have my phone. Brett smashed it in front of me. Jin will be insane with worry. I'm worried about Aunt Clara. How will they know what medications to give her? Is she worried that I didn't stop by? Where did Ellen and Stefan go?

At school, I gingerly step out, closing my eyes and leaning against the car. It's over. I'm not sure what to do next. I don't think I can run. Not with Father possibly putting Aunt Clara in danger.

I smell his warmth before I hear him. "Ara." Rory is there. "I texted you last night, but you didn't reply," he murmurs. "I want to walk you to class." His arms encircle me as he nuzzles my neck.

I squeak, wincing. When Rory pulls away in confusion, I whisper, "I'm not used to public displays of affection."

His brow clears, but he grabs my hand instead. "You'll have to get used to. I'm telling the whole school you're mine," he says smugly.

I want to laugh, but I can't. My walk feels unnatural and stiff. I feel students' eyes on us, but Rory continues confidently.

"I'll see you in math class," he murmurs, stroking my cheek with a finger.

Desperately, I hug him. I have a bad feeling about what will happen to me when I get back to Aunt Clara's. "Rory, please find Jin for me."

Rory bewilderment shows, but the bell rings. "We'll talk about it later," he promises.

Emily is grinning when I sit down gingerly. "Hmm, one Paris Dumonte is going to be in a very bad mood. Rory's never held hands with a girl or shown affection."

"Thank you," I tell her, "for being such a good friend."

Emily just laughs. I manage to get through class, and Emily begins to notice my lack of energy. During second period, I'm lagging even more. Suddenly, the teacher calls my name. "You're wanted in the office, Laura."

When I stand, I weave. Emily catches me. "Sir, can I walk her to the office? I think she's not feeling well." The teacher nods and waves us out.

I'm grateful for her help. My legs feel heavy and unnatural.

"Laura, are you okay? You're so pale. You're sweating." Emily's dark eyes are worried.

I pause right before I get to the office. "I'm glad we met. If – If I don't return to class, tell Rory not to forget."

Emily's worry increases. "Laura, what's going on?"

I look over my shoulder as the main office door opens. I see my father and my throat goes dry. I hug her. "My father."

When I pull back, Emily is stricken with fear and worry for me.

"Laura," my father begins, "it'd be best if you come with me now. Let's not make a fuss. Your aunt passed away this morning. With your medical history, and with your latest behavior, we're very concerned that this added stress will be too difficult for you to handle." He grabs my arm.

I already know what this means. They're going to send me back.

On the drive, I'm numb. Aunt Clara is dead. She's gone. Father looks at me in the mirror. Brett sits next to me to make sure I don't do anything dumb.

"I'll give you everything," I promise. "Please don't do this."

"There you go again with histrionics," Father scolds me. "We're trying to protect you from yourself."

"I won't say anything. You can have the money. I don't want it."

"I'm filing a motion to have guardianship and conservatorship transferred to me due to your delicate mental state even after you're eighteen," Father informs me. "It's important we get you adequate medical care."

I stare at him. "Please don't do this."

When we get to the treatment facility, I fight. I scream. I tell the doctors my father is a liar. I tell them to check my back. But no one listens. When they sedate me, they ignore my cries. When the darkness envelops me, I give up.

RORY

CHAPTER 15

When Laura doesn't show up in math class, I know something's wrong. Her behavior niggled at me all morning. I text her a few times, but I get nothing. By the time class is done, I'm about to explode.

Paris gives me a sultry smile as I storm the hallways. "Looking for your sweet Laura?" Her eyes narrow cruelly. "I told the staff that I saw her try to kill herself."

"You did what?!" I bare my teeth at her, pushing her into the wall. I'm ready to rip her throat out.

"She's sick," Paris says, face pale with fear.

"I am going to break your neck!" I growl. But then Emily finds me, Kenji hulking over her shoulder with worry. I release Paris and watch her scurry away like a weasel.

"Laura… Her father showed up and took her," Emily says, and I can see that she knows that Laura's father is bad news. Her lips tremble. "Laura looked scared."

I don't wait. I race to Laura's home and pound on the door. I'm about to break the door down when a gardener tells me that the coroner took Clara Atherton's body away already and that the family hasn't been back since this morning.

Shit. Clara Atherton is dead. I go home, screaming for Blake.

"What the hell, Rory?" My brother comes down the steps. I told him everything last night, about Laura and her father.

"They took her!"

Blake frowns. He's been through hell with the accusations, but he's always been the calmer of the two of us. "Shit, Rory, what are you talking about?"

"They took Ara! Her father!" I try to unscramble my words. "Her aunt died this morning. I knew something was off about her behavior! Her father came and took her!"

"Calm down," Blake says. "They're probably arranging the funeral and stuff. Call her later."

"No!" I say it with absolute certainty. "Her father is a fucking lunatic, Blake. Do you think he's going to let his daughter inherit Clara Atherton's fortune? She knows what really happened to Marigold Summers!"

Blake pales as he follows my train of thought. He cares about Laura. Even after what happened, he never held it against her, saying she must've been mistaken. I was the one who held a grudge. And for no good reason.

"Blake, I can't fucking lose her!" My hands twist into Blake's shirt. Once upon a time, he was bigger and taller. Now, we're the same height, but I'm stronger.

"Rory Remington!" my mother scolds, coming into the room. "Your school just called because you left without permission! And you're here, swearing up a storm!"

"Fuck school!" I scream at her. "Laura's missing, Mom! God, what if they're hurting her?" I remember her yelp this morning and close my eyes. I'm such a fucking idiot. She was hurt. They hurt her. My Ara. I told her I'd protect her.

Blake tries to explain things to Mom, but I can't stay still. I think of all the time I wasted with useless anger. I cringe at every horrible thing I said to her. I planned to make it up to her, cherish her, love her.

"Where would they take Laura? Eventually, they'll bring her back to her aunt's," Mom says reasonably. "I'll get in touch with our lawyer. We'll see what we can do to free her from her father. It'll be alright."

"Mom. I can't go back to school. Not until Ara's back with me. Mom," I choke out, and suddenly I fall to my knees in helpless anger. "She's important."

I think I want you to be my first kiss. I knew then. When I said those words to her that February. I knew that I would never love anyone else but her.

Mom has never liked Laura's father or mother. She found them strange. She thought it was odd that Laura and Jin were picture perfect. They sat. They never wiggled. They never spoke unless spoken to. My memories complete a picture I never saw. Jin would grab Laura's hand whenever Brett would talk to them. Protective. Reassuring. Laura's face when her father spoke to her. The strange rules.

Mom hugs me. "You love her," she whispers. "But you need to calm down. Let me first contact the school. I'll tell them it's an emergency. God knows, I give them enough money. They'll give us leeway. Then I'll call our lawyer and see what we can do. If Laura's willing to tell the court that her father is abusive, we can legally emancipate her."

"She'll do it. I'll make her," I swear. Once she knows she's safe, I'm sure she'll do what's necessary.

For a moment, I brighten. Legal emancipation. She'll be free from her father. I'll take a gap year when I graduate. We'll get Jin out, too. Laura won't leave without him.

There's a commotion at the front door, and Blake and I head over to investigate. Even if we hadn't been best friends as kids, I would know him because he has Laura's eyes. At our doorway is an older woman and Jin, Laura's twin, looking like his world has ended.

Jin's beyond exhausted. The moment he heard his father was here, he'd used his money to buy a one-way ticket. Ellen, the gray-haired woman who had been dismissed the moment Lionel Atherton showed up, knew something was amiss. She was the one who'd called Jin on Sunday.

Blake gives Jin some water while my mother listens to Ellen. Ellen had long suspected that Laura's father was abusive. Her descriptions of Laura's fears and initial timidity make me flinch, but Jin remains numb and drained. When Clara Atherton realized the cancer treatments were ineffective, her hopeful timeline of eighteen months had been shortened to less than eight. She'd started the process of requesting guardianship of Laura to finish the school year at Cove. But she'd died before completion.

Something about Ellen's words make me wonder if Clara died due to cancer or something else.

When Jin finally speaks, he sounds older than he looks. He's almost too pretty to be a boy. "What did she tell you, Rory?" he asks, his eyes emotionless.

"I think everything." I pause and then shake my head. I'm not sure. I wanted to give her time to adjust to things before questioning her further.

"The hospitalizations?" He notices my surprise with a wry twist of his mouth. "Thought not. Why do you think I've been waiting for us to turn eighteen? You don't think I've been trying to get us out?"

Blake places his elbows on his knees. "What hospitalizations?"

Rory's face contorts with guilt and grief. "They kept us apart after Father made her talk to the police. When she realized what was happening, she was determined to tell you the truth. She tried to get to you, Rory, and she thought you'd protect her. She crept out her bedroom window." With a shaky hand, he covers his face. "Brett caught her. He – He dropped her from the second floor. That's why you never saw her again. The fall broke her leg."

My heart breaks into a million pieces. She'd tried. Jin's words cut into me. She wanted me to protect her, and I wasn't there. What kind of brother drops his sister like that? I think of her, broken, trying to reach me. Blake is equally devastated. My mom just clutches a hand to her heart.

"Father told the doctors that she was suicidal and had become violent." Jin keeps shaking his head. "I'll never know if they did something to make her seem more irrational, but when they let me see her, she was feral, paranoid, terrified. When she came home, finally, she was so fragile. To keep me under control, Father threatened her. Brett threatened her. She was a shadow, barely existing. Two years ago, she tried to kill herself. They locked her up again. Father declared her mentally incompetent. She's been careful, but she has triggers." Jin begins to cry a little. "You see, when I'm eighteen, I can have a judge make me her guardian. We just need to make it until I can do that."

I want to throw up. The car. "She tried to jump off a building," I say dumbly. With shame, I add, "I goaded someone to scratch her car. She – snapped.

Panicked. She ran."

I expect Jin to yell at me or get angry, but his expression remains sad. "As I said, she has triggers. I've done a lot of research about it. It's PTSD." He turns to Blake. "She never meant any of that to happen, Blake. I swear. She's been through so much. She's taken the brunt of the pain and punishment. It's not just Father. Brett's psychotic. He'd torment her."

"Did he touch her?" I need to hit something. If Jin says yes, I'm killing Brett the moment I see him. I'll go to jail if it means he can't torment her anymore.

Jin says, "I don't know. I don't think so. She would've told me, I think. But he – he says a lot of things that are perverse, sick, and twisted. I taught her ways to lock her door so he couldn't come in at night."

What kind of life has Laura lived? Locking her door? I'm going to kill him. It'll take me away from Laura, but it'll be worth it. Blake puts a hand on my shoulder. "Jin," he says, "I was never angry at her. She was twelve." The look he gives me is borderline caustic. "I wish she'd known she could have come to us. We would've found a way…"

Ellen interjects softly, "You think they're going to put her in a psychiatric ward, don't you?"

"I think they already have," Jin whispers.

CHAPTER 16

It takes two days to find Laura. Mom pulls in every favor and we finally get a lead. Mr. Townshend, our family lawyer, gets an emergency court order to have her re-evaluated by a different doctor. Armed with a court order, my mother drives me and Jin to the facility.

Mr. Townshend is already there with a sheriff, securing her release. I've never wanted to kiss a guy before, but I come close when I see the discharge papers.

A nurse wheels Laura out, and I become breathless with rage. Her face is expressionless – when Jin cries out her name, she remains oblivious. I want to hit every doctor and nurse I see. Instead, I push the nurse out of the way and pick her up in my arms. Jin warns the staff the stay away. He's slighter than me, but there is a lean strength to him.

"Ara, love, I'm here," I whisper to her in the car. It's cold, and she's dressed in some weird hospital gown, but Jin grabs the blanket I brought, and we tuck it around her as well as we can. I know Jin wants to check her, too, but I can't let her go. I have to hold her or I'll break. She stays, unresponsive, on my lap while I whisper reassurances to her.

I take her to my room even though my mom's askance looks tells me she doesn't think it's appropriate. I don't care. The doctor arrives and Mom gives him the discharge papers. The look on his face speaks volumes. He doesn't approve of what was done to her.

We lie on the bed. Laura in the middle with me on one side and Jin on the other. Jin, face-to-face, softly speaks to her while I curl myself around her back, breathing in her presence. When the doctor comes, he asks for alone time with Laura. I snarl, possessive as fuck. He assures me the nurse will be with him and it will only be for about ten minutes.

The only reason I agree with it is that Jin agrees. I look at Laura longingly, willing her to wake up, but she doesn't move.

Mr. Townshend is outlining legal possibilities for Laura to my mom. Her father will have to grab her out of my dead hands if he wants her.

"Judges tend to favor biological parents when it comes to guardianship," he tells us. "Her father has clearly put some thought into this. He's documented it in such a way that proving Laura is capable of representing herself is tricky. The only guardianship that outweighs parental rights is that of a spouse."

My head snaps up. "Spouse?"

"Hypothetically, a spouse has more authority than a parent, but obviously she's not married." Our lawyer laughs a little.

"What if she got married?" I stare at Jin. "What if I married her? I'm eighteen."

"Rory, are you out of your mind?" Jin asks in alarm.

Blake puts a hand on my mom's arm, requesting patience. I forge ahead. "Tell me, Mr. Townshend, what would it take for us to get married?"

Our lawyer responds uneasily, "Well, the bride has to be willing. But since she's seventeen, it would need sign off from a judge – or at last one parent's consent."

"Find a judge," I snap.

"Rory, wait," Mom begins.

I shake my head. "No, I'll ask her myself—"

"Wait a minute, man," Jin sputters. "I appreciate your willingness, but –"

"I love her, Jin. I've always loved her." I put my hand on his shoulder. "I won't push her for anything. If, after a year, she wants it, I'll divorce her. If she doesn't say yes, we'll find another way. I'm not crazy, but I'll be damned if they take her away from me."

Jin stares at me. "Rory, Aunt Clara left her everything. My father gets nothing if he doesn't keep her."

"By the time he gets anything in motion, she'll be eighteen, and with a spouse, she'd have time to prove herself mentally competent," Mr. Townshend says. "Her father wouldn't have legal grounds to pursue anything."

"Find a judge," I say again. I've been away from Laura for too long. I ignore the look from Mom.

Jin's right on my heels when I get back to my room. The doctor is finishing up. "They gave her a drug that makes her compliant but unresponsive. Apparently, it was for hysteria, but it seems like she was fighting to get out. It should wear off in a few hours. I'd like to evaluate her in two days to determine if she actually needs medication."

Over my dead body. But I nod as Jin settles beside his sister, holding her hands between his. As soon as the doctor leaves, I join them, cuddling up to her backside. I take easy breaths knowing I have her now. I fall asleep, my heart safe in my arms.

Whispering wakes me: Laura's softer voice mingling with her brother's deeper one. They're hushed in my darkened room.

"When do you have to leave?" she asks Jin.

"I'm not. I'm staying with you. This isn't temporary, Ara."

"I'm sorry for causing trouble," she whispers.

Instinctively I move, pulling her close. I can't bear to hear her blame herself. "No, love, it's not your fault." I kiss her head, relishing the sound of her voice. She doesn't pull away either. My heart pounds like crazy in my chest. "Does your back still hurt? Do you need anything?" For that alone, I'd kill them.

"It's okay. A little tender," she says. "Is it true? Jin can stay?"

"Ara, Aunt Clara left everything to you," Jin says. "Ellen told me Aunt Clara changed her will. You get everything."

Instead of being happy, her voice goes flat. "I don't want it. Tell Father he can have it all if he leaves us alone."

"Jin, can I speak to your sister alone?" I know I could just tell her what I want to do, but it sounds cold and calculating just to ask her in front of her twin. She deserves something more epic. I feel her tense, a small whimper at the thought of her brother leaving, and it stings. I'm starting to doubt my plan, which is based on the presumption that she feels something for me.

"I'm hungry, Ara. After you talk to Rory, come down. We can raid the fridge." The way Jin says it, it sounds like a reference to a special memory between the two of them. I shouldn't be jealous, but I am.

When we're alone, I press soft kisses to her head and then her neck. "Do you remember our first kiss?" I whisper. "The snow clung to your lashes. Your lips were soft but cold. It felt both forbidden and cool at the same time. My first kiss."

"I remember."

"You had my heart five years ago, Ara. I love you." I hear her breath catch. "Your father – we now know what he'll do to you out of greed. He won't stop because you're the only one that knows the truth about what happened to Marigold."

"I know."

"Marry me. If you marry me, your conservatorship and guardianship would be transferred to me as your spouse." She tenses in my arms, and I curse inwardly. "I wouldn't use it against you. It would just be on paper to protect you." I stroke her hair, wishing she'd say something. "Laura, I'd marry you even without the threat of your father. I know – I know it requires you to trust me."

"You want to get married?" She sounds confused.

I really botched up the asking part. "Laura, I know you've suffered. I'd do anything to make that suffering go away. But I swear, if you marry me, I'll show you what it's like to be loved. And if, after a year, I can't make you happy, we can get a divorce, no hard feelings." It would devastate me, but she doesn't need to know that.

"Marriage means…" She trails off, squirming uncomfortably.

I'm such an asshole. With the crap her father has dumped on her, of course, she'd be uncomfortable about sex. "We don't have to have sex," I whisper. "I wouldn't demand it." I hate that I'm saying it, but it's true. I'd never force her. "You'd have full authority over that aspect. But," again she tenses in my arms, "I want to share a bed. And I want to be able to kiss you."

I'm relieved when she relaxes at my requirements. I've never been unsure of my abilities to persuade a girl before, but she's not just any girl. Laura's quiet for a long time – maybe I've overestimated her feelings for me. I think about how she reacts. She doesn't flinch when I touch her. She's responsive when we kiss.

"You deserve a huge wedding," I continue, "but we'll do something small and private for now. A Christmas wedding. Snowflakes on our cake. Jin will give you away. I'll take you away for spring break. We'll eat chocolate bonbons in bed. Get massages. I'll spoil you with lavish dinners." She giggles and my heart lightens. "We'll stay up late watching movies. I'll take you shopping. We can buy matching pajamas." I kiss her ear softly. "Please marry me. I'll be content just to be near you, and your father will never touch you again."

Even in the dark, I can see the glimmer of her eyes when she faces me. "I'll marry you."

CHAPTER 17

I pick out Laura's engagement ring with care. I choose a Harry Winston cushion-cut sapphire ring set in platinum. The sapphire is the color of my eyes. Jin thinks it's way too much symbolism and tells me I have an ego bigger than the sun. The wedding bands are matching platinum bands, but hers has a single 0.04 carat round diamond. I have it brought to us by courier, cost be damned.

We secure a judge to approve the marriage and waive the permissions. I never ask how my mom and our lawyer make it happen. I don't think Laura's one of those girls that fantasize about their wedding for years, but if she wants a fancy wedding, she can have it next year. Right now, I care only about the paper making her my wife in the eyes of the law.

A befuddled Emily and Kenji are invited, and I also invite Jaylen and Zyair.

"You're getting married?" Zyair says to me, scratching his chin when I make him show up in a suit.

"Yes. Today. Keep the smart comments to yourself."

"Okay, and who are you marrying?" my friend asks.

"Laura Atherton."

Jaylen spews his drink. "Holy shit. I knew you liked her but isn't this kind of fast?"

If looks could kill... "It's a long and complicated story. She's mine. Period. And, Zyair?"

"Yeah?"

"Don't ever ogle her again." I look at Jaylen. "And don't dance with her again unless you ask me first." Jaylen opens his mouth. "She isn't pregnant, asshole."

"You're fucking serious," Zyair says to me, his dark eyes wide.

I stare at my friends. "I am. Mom and Dad both think I'm nuts, but they also know I'm not changing my mind." They're not opposed to Laura. They're worried I'm rushing Laura into a situation she isn't ready to handle.

Emily walks over to me. "I think she's ready to come down." There's this expression on her face that tells me Kenji is ready to kill me if I hurt Laura. It won't happen, but I'm glad Laura has a fierce friend.

Jaylen and Zyair sit down near Ellen. Stefan, the bulky guy next to Ellen, even made us a cake with snowflakes. I already have our lawyer kicking the

Athertons out tomorrow – I would be there, but I'm sure if I saw either Brett or Laura's father, I'd be arrested for murder. Ellen will go in and make sure the place is secure – it's now Laura's, and it's going to be our home.

There's rustling as the county clerk who's marrying us gets ready. And then Laura appears, her brother Jin at her side. I'm not sure where she found the dress – it isn't your typical wedding dress – but it's perfect. It's an ivory sheath dress according to my mother, and I know it's my imagination, but she glows.

You'd know Jin and Laura are related just by looking at them side by side. Kenji, who is the most experimental guy I know, gave Jin the look – the one that says he'd willingly experiment with Jin given the chance. Jin and I had a long talk this morning – the kind of talk only a brother or a father who gave a damn would give. Some threats, some promises, but mostly reestablishing our relationship. Five years ago, they let me join them: the new kid without friends befriending the twins who couldn't have friends. It's fitting that Jin gives his sister away.

As the clerk goes through the ceremony, I can't stop looking at her. Her eyes are lowered – shy or nervous – but her hands are steady when we join them. Her responses are calm and cool. I slide the band on her finger and there's a primal surge within me. She's mine. Incontrovertibly. Our kiss is chaste, sweet.

I let Dad deal with the paperwork and make a copy for our lawyer. I let Blake kiss Laura on the cheek. And then I savor the moment, pressing my forehead to hers.

Our miniature reception involves mostly relaxed conversations, amazing appetizers, and wedding cake which Laura and I feed to each other. Jaylen and Zyair haven't met Jin before, and since I'm so absorbed with my newly minted wife, I don't see them chatting amicably until much later.

I take a moment to talk to my parents. "Mom, Dad, I know you're freaked out by this, but I appreciate you both letting me do what I need to do."

Mom admits, "It's borderline insane. But I know that face. The moment the suggestion came about, you were determined to make it happen."

Dad just looks at me. "Marriage is a lot of work, Rory. If you go into that knowing that it's not always easy, you'll be better equipped for dealing with the challenges."

Jin drives us to the pretty resort where I've rented the honeymoon suite. I have a real honeymoon planned for spring break, but I'm not spending the first night as a married man under my parents' roof.

Once we're in the room, I pick her up and deposit her on the bed, kissing her thoroughly. It's highly satisfying. She's nervous as I slowly unzip her dress. She keeps her back towards me, and I do my best not to gawk as I remove the dress, as I take my time exposing her back inch by inch. The bruising from her father is faint, but it reignites my rage. There are other marks, too. A few scars which I touch tenderly. I force myself to be calm, running my knuckles against her shoulder blades. It's deliberately intimate and sensuous – I want her to feel desire and know she's desirable. She shivers when my hand grazes her skin as the dress falls to the floor. My breathing deepens and quickens.

I want more, but she's not ready for more. I won't be another person who abuses her trust. As promised, I bought matching pajamas – Christmas-themed with candy canes and trees. Her laugh is breathless as I slip it over her head, doing the little buttons until she's demure and adorable. And then I change out of my clothes. She peeks at me a few times, shy and with color high on her cheeks. When I'm in my matching pair, I turn her around, and I smile when she giggles. I'd do anything to keep that smile on her face.

We climb into bed with chocolate bonbons, and I let her pick the movie. I love that she surprises me by choosing *Deadpool*. It's a perfect finger to her father. She curls up against me, smelling of peaches, her laughter a mix of shock and wicked mirth. I've never loved her more.

Clara Asherton is laid to rest in an urn next to her husband. The only ones present are me, my parents, Blake, Laura, Jin, Clara's household staff, and Emily and her brother Kenji. Laura sheds a few tears for the woman who, at the very last minute, decided enough was enough. Ellen and Stefan weep for the woman and friend. The rest of us are here for Laura and Jin.

I watch Laura stand next to her brother; their hands are clasped in solidarity. In a black dress which she would never have been allowed to wear, there's a delicate strength about her. She may see herself as weak, but no person who understands the mental and physical torture she's endured would think that. She's strong – strong enough to make a desperately needed friend, strong enough to be willing to tell me some of her truth, strong enough to feel the tenuous threads of physical desire. I could claim, in my vanity, it's me and my highly desirable body. But it's more than that. Laura's never been weak. She's just been biding her time.

CHAPTER 18

Getting Jin enrolled at Cove was as simple as writing a check. Our first day back to school after the winter break and I'm the last one in the kitchen. My wife is chatting with her twin, their dark heads bent together like they're conspiring. Heaven help us if they really are conspiring. Stefan, who moved in last week, is busily piling food onto plates.

The place is too big for just two people. I want Laura to feel safe, so we filled it with people who she loves and trusts. It makes sense that Blake is here. They're both coming to terms with the horrors of the past. With how much Blake and I eat, having Stefan here made sense.

Blake runs in to grab a muffin before heading to the room he's commandeered as his office, shouting, "Have fun at school!"

Stefan hands me a mug of coffee as I sit down beside Laura. Her cheeks have color, her lips are curved, and her eyes are bright. I take her coffee out of her hand and lift her so she's on my lap. I ignore Jin's eye roll as I nuzzle her. When she stands up to grab some fruit, I'm glad she can't read minds since a few dirty thoughts cross my mind when I check her out in her uniform.

Jin's aligned his classes so he's with his sister in almost every class but gym. The boys and girls remain separated during gym class. Call it sexism, but no one has done a thing to change it. I drop Laura off at her first class, acknowledging Emily with a nod. Students' eyes are on us when I kiss her. She's still getting used to the PDA, but the wedding ring on her hand is hard to hide. I'm smug as I release her. There's no mistaking my claim.

Jaylen and Zyair share my first period. "So, how was she in bed?" Zyair asks.

"None of your fucking business." My smile is sharp. "I'm not discussing *my wife* with either of you."

Jaylen leans back to observe me. "You're happy. It's going to be weird not seeing your grumpy face all the time."

Whipped as I am, I text Laura in between classes, trying to fight a grin when she texts me back right away. Jaylen hisses a warning when Paris enters, her eyes livid.

"I come to school and some fucking piece of shit tells me you're married, Rory," she spits out, her red lips twisted with rage.

I hold up my hand so she can see the ring. "Yup. Laura's my wife."

Paris sucks in her breath. "How can you do this to me? I did what you wanted. You said she was a whore."

I slam my hand on the table. "Don't call her that. I know you hit her! You will not touch her again. Now get out of my face." I stand up, letting all the menace into my face. "Or do I need to make you leave?"

Paris pales and backs off, but I'm in a foul mood. I'd been so wrapped up with Laura's father that I'd overlooked the drama queens at the school. I won't have anyone hurting her.

When Laura arrives in math class with her twin, I stand up when several guys look her way. They immediately find something else more interesting. Laura misses my jealous fit, but Jin just cocks a brow at me, trying not to smirk.

At lunch, we draw the eyes of boys and girls alike. I won't make Laura sit at the Idols' table with Paris, so I join her and Emily. Several girls stop by, ostensibly to offer us their congratulations, but when they primp in front of Jin, I cover my smirk. With the popularity of K-pop, Jin is in a mess of trouble. Jaylen and Zyair frown at our circle. Paris, Stacy, and Deanna glare. Gauging everyone's reactions, I have a feeling that Jaylen and Zyair will be abandoning those girls sooner rather than later.

There are more than a few curious stares. How often does one leave for break and come back married? Laura shifts uncomfortably.

"Hey, look at me," I say to her softly, waiting until her dark brown eyes meet mine. "They're just wondering how I snagged the prettiest girl in school."

"They think I'm pregnant," she says sourly, and I huff in laughter.

"They'll see soon enough that you're not." Not to mention that, unless Laura plans to be the next Virgin Mary, we haven't had sex. Yet.

Her twin is more relaxed as he glances around casually. "What's up with the baleful looks from that table?" he asks, gesturing to the Idols' table.

Paris has not stopped glaring, her petulant mouth frozen in a frown. Her eyes narrow as she decides to move towards us, deliberately swinging her hips.

"Laura," she tries to purr, but her voice just grates on my nerves, "introduce me to your brother."

The thing about Jin is that he can spot a bully a mile away. He stands, extending his hand so that Laura doesn't need to speak. "Jin. We're twins."

"Mmm. I see the masculine resemblance," she coos, the insult falling so flat that I'm surprised she deigned to say it.

"Piss off, Paris," Emily scoffs, "no one wants to hear your vapid comments."

"Did Rory tell you, Laura? He got me to come after you." Paris becomes sharp and vicious. "The locker. Gym class. He laughed. And you fucking married your bully. You must like abuse. Oh, I know, you're a masochist!"

The digs hit Laura hard, not because they're true but because of the abuse she's suffered. I stand up, ready to hit Paris.

She continues, "Do you let him do it rough? He likes it rough, you know. I should know. Last year—"

I move, grabbing Paris by the arm and twisting it viciously behind her back. "You keep your fucking mouth shut!" I snap at her.

Jaylen and Zyair walk towards us. If they defend Paris, I will take them out.

"Don't," Laura whispers. "Don't hurt her."

God, her words cut. I let Paris go, turning to Laura. Her limpid eyes lower as she clutches her brother's hand for comfort.

"Paris, you're done," Jaylen says quietly. "Back off."

The bitch's voice rings out, "She deserves to know. Ask him how many girls he's—"

She never finishes because Zyair picks her up like a fireman and takes her outside.

"Ara, love," I say softly, extending my hand. She doesn't flinch, but she turns away. It stings. "Laura, we'll talk about this later, okay? I have a past. Not a pretty one. But it has nothing to do with us."

"Jin." One word, one look. Twin talk. Her brother takes her arm and helps her stand.

I'm not letting them abandon me in the lunchroom. I follow them out, even though Emily makes this gesture at me to stay. In the hallway, away from prying eyes, I growl, "Laura."

She goes still. Jin tells me to stop. "Rory, give her some space. I get the queen bitch is trying to rile things up, but that doesn't make it any easier."

Give her space? Haven't I given her space? I've made no demands of her body or her affection. I don't expect her to love me – at least, not yet – but it'd be nice to know she cares. I don't push because she's been manipulated her whole life. She doesn't need me to guilt her into love.

We've never talked about my previous relationships – to be honest, I haven't had anything I would call a relationship. I've had a string of mainly one-night stands. I do it for one thing: pure physical release. In the scope of things, it doesn't seem that important.

I'm resentful. Frustrated. Reduced. "Fine," I nearly snap.

The twins can mope around each other. It's childish, I know. But I can't help myself. I take my wounded pride and go to class.

CHAPTER 19

Jaylen texts me to say he'll try and keep Paris off Laura. I feel like I'm in middle school again. Annoyance hits me hard when I spy Laura resting her head on her twin's shoulder during the drive home. She wouldn't even sit in the front with me.

Since fifteen, I haven't wanted for attention or partners. Maybe that makes me a pig. I guess I never imagined I would return to a certain dark-eyed girl I kissed even if the memory of her haunted me every day.

I don't speak to the twins when we reach home. I head straight to the bedroom – our bedroom – and take a shower. I need to clear my head. Is she going to ignore me all night, too? When did I become so needy?

I towel myself off, more determined to make her talk to me. Wrapping the towel around my waist, I head towards the closet, freezing when I see Laura on the bed. She's sitting cross-legged, a piece of paper in her hand, staring at me with wide eyes. Her pink cheeks make me wonder what thoughts cross her mind. I continue on to the closet, dropping the towel when my back is to her before slipping clothes on. It's an asshole move of letting her get an eyeful. When I turn to her, her eyes are demurely lowered. Maybe it didn't work.

"We should talk about what happened earlier today," I say, not letting her speak first, "because I don't want it to fester between us."

Her mouth makes a little moue, but she keeps her eyes averted.

I sit on the bed. "I slept with Paris last year. Once. I've had many one-night stands. But this – you and me – it's never going to be a one-night stand. If I wanted a one-night thing with you, I certainly wouldn't have married you. You're my first real relationship, and the only one that matters."

"How many? How many one-night stands? How many jealous girls do I have to contend with?"

I scowl. "Twenty?" I'm not sure. Definitely not more than thirty.

"So, I should try about twenty to thirty guys before I settle with you?" she asks archly.

I scowl even more. "No. Don't even joke about it, Laura." Jealousy rips through me. Is there someone she'd even consider over me?

"Jaylen seems nice," she continues with a shrug.

I move, pinning her to the bed. "I said don't joke," I snarl, gripping her tightly. She starts to shake. What am I doing? I swear inwardly, ready to apologize. But then I realize she's shaking with laughter. "Laura?" She tries to look solemn and fails.

"It's a bit unfair, don't you think? What if you're not very good?"

If I'm not very good? This playful side is unexpected. But I'm not opposed to it. I carefully move my body to cover hers. "That sounds like a challenge, Ara." I take my time kissing her, getting lost in the moment. When my fingers graze her thigh, I sense the change in her and stop.

"I wasn't upset about Paris. Or even the other girls." She makes a face. "No, I'm a little upset. Paris doesn't seem very nice. And I know... I know about the car and..." She trails off.

I feel like a monster. "You have no idea how sorry I am. Ara, sweetheart, I swear—"

"Teach me how to defend myself," she says, interrupting. "I'm tired of cowering." Her brow furrows. "I'm tired of people thinking I'm weak and pathetic." Her voice rises as she continues to speak.

"Ara, love, you –"

Her face becomes stubborn. "Don't you get it? I'm sick of it!" Her teeth snap together as her face flushes with anger. "People look at me like I'm broken! I don't need to be fixed! I need to get strong! I wasn't upset because of your damn past or that you screwed everything with a vagina!"

"Hey!"

Her fists pummel my chest. "I was mad because everyone thinks they have to protect me!"

I twist to grab her wrists and pin them down. "Okay. I'll teach you. But only on two conditions." I love her suspicious frown. "One, you work with me and the people I pick. And two, you can only train when I'm around." Oh, the eye roll. "Laura, I'm serious. I went mad when your father took you. So, bear with me if I'm a little overprotective."

"Fine." Her look is eager. "When do we start?"

"Tomorrow."

"It's a good idea," Blake opines when I mention it to him. But I'm here to talk to him about something else.

Laura's working on homework – she kicked me out because I was distracting her. I receive no sympathy from Jin or Blake.

"It's hard to curb my impulses," Jin admits, trying to make me feel better. "We've been preconditioned to think of girls as the weaker sex. You know, I hated being parted from Ara, but Father unknowingly helped us. Ara would never have said anything if I'd been here. I got a job, started karate because I didn't have to worry about Laura's safety." He closes his eyes briefly, and the tension drops from his face.

I clear my throat. "Blake, Laura received a letter this afternoon... We've been looking for Marigold Summers." The paper which got crumpled when I pressed her to the bed… "We found her. Laura wants to talk to her."

Blake looks like he might be sick. In the five years since that night, Blake has gone from outgoing to reclusive, and nothing we do can revert his life to what it was before. "What would be the point?" he asks bitterly. "Atherton washed any possible DNA away. Marigold never saw her attacker. The only possible witness is Laura."

Jin unravels his body from the chair. "Marigold has a right to know what really happened." Laura's twin moves to the window, staring into the dark. "It's a sense of closure for Marigold. It's clearing your name. It's closure for Ara, too. A lot changed that night. For you, for Rory, for me, for Ara."

Blake rubs a weary hand over his face before answering. "We won't get any of our lives back, Jin. I've tried to let it go. There were no official charges."

"Letting it go means their father wins, Blake," I say irritably. "I won't stop Laura if this is what she needs, but she won't do it if she thinks it'll hurt you."

"Just – let me think about it." Blake stands abruptly and leaves.

I exhale heavily. "Do I need to ask how you're doing, Jin?"

Jin chuckles darkly, glancing at me over his shoulder. "My sister just became filthy rich, I'm free from my psychotic family, and I'm attending a fancy school." He returns to his study of the darkness. "What do I have to complain about?" he asks cynically. "My weakness? My inability to protect her?"

"You gave her emotional strength. Hope."

Jin faces me. "For what it's worth, I'm glad you two found each other again. You made her brave back then. The only sad thing is that," he pauses for dramatic effect, "you're whipped. You let me deal with my demons, Rory. Help Ara with hers."

I climb back to the bedroom, smiling to myself. Laura's fallen asleep, hand curled beneath her cheek, her pose nearly childlike. Carefully, I close her laptop and then settle her beneath the covers. I crawl in next to her, holding her close. She sighs, stirring briefly in my arms. Yeah, I'm whipped.

CHAPTER 20

Jaylen watches Kenji pin Laura to the mat while Emily provides feedback. "Notice your lack of leverage when your hands are pinned that way," she points out. "Laura, move your hands to where Kenji shows you. You need leverage to flip him over."

"When you work with Laura, I'll be watching," I tell Jaylen in a menacing tone.

"Afraid I'll get handsy?" he taunts.

I smack the back of his head. "No, because then I'd rip off your dick. I'll pummel you if she gets hurt."

Jaylen smirks. "So, that's why you handed off kickboxing to me. Don't want to get rough with your girl."

There are other reasons. It'd kill me if she got scared of me during training. I'm also leery of having her body squirming beneath mine. I've been a saint with Laura, and I don't need her seeing how quickly my body reacts to hers.

Truth be told, I'm anxious for spring break. I'm taking Laura to Bora Bora for our official honeymoon where I hope the privacy, romantic dinners, and excessive wooing on my part will make her keen on consummation. At the very least, maybe she'll fall in love with me.

Kenji's been a trooper with Laura. With his wrestling skills, he knows how to break holds better than anyone. Initially, I'd been concerned Laura would panic at being pinned. But she's taken everything in stride.

On the other side of the gym, Zyair is working with Jin. Jin's naturally fast on his feet, so Zyair's teaching him sparring techniques. I'm not sure how much Jaylen's guessed about the twins, but he's more intuitive than I am. He'd noticed early on that Laura was skittish.

It's been weeks since Paris had her outburst. I'd love to say that I wouldn't use violence or hit a woman, but when it comes to Laura, I'd cross a lot of lines.

"Hey, been meaning to ask you… You and Jin call Laura 'Ara' sometimes. Some sort of Asian thing?" Jaylen asks.

"It can mean several things in Korean," I explain. "Knowledge. Goodness. Beautiful. It's part of her middle name and JIn said he thought it captured his sister perfectly."

"Hello. Would you like to be our friend?"

"I don't have any friends here."

"We're not allowed to have many friends. It makes perfect sense to have a friend who doesn't have any friends. That way, I'll never have to worry about having too many friends."

Even back then, her voice got to me. I can remember the precision in her words, the quiet way she reached out to me, the way she pulled me to her.

Laura's extricates herself to Kenji's satisfaction. He gestures Jaylen to join them. They work through several scenarios to test Laura's competency. She's focused and fierce, and I watch with pride as she tackles each challenge. I check the time and signal everyone to wrap it up.

Face glowing, Laura runs to me, faintly sweaty and flushed. I'm surprised when she initiates the kiss, but I'm certainly willing to go along with it. Dressed in an oversized shirt and sweats, she's still beautiful.

Jin and Zyair chat amicably as they rejoin our group. "Sweetheart Dance, Jin. Girls want to know who you're asking," Zyair chortles.

"Yeah, now that Rory's an old married man, you're the school's latest fascination," Jaylen points out, ignoring Jin's dismay.

"I'm hungry," Laura announces. She'd been downright bony in December, so her words are music to my ears. She's still too thin, but her skin has a healthier tone and her face isn't gaunt anymore.

"Have you thought about what you're going to do after Cove Prep?" Jaylen inquires, his question more for Laura than for me.

Laura slides her glance towards me as I put a possessive hand at her waist. "I'll wait for Laura to graduate. I applied to several schools in early fall. If none of them appeal to her, we'll pick one together."

That little secret smile of hers emerges – it either means I'm putty in her hands or that she's happy about my response. Or maybe it's both.

CHAPTER 21

I'm not typically romantic – remember, no real relationships, just a lot of hookups. Valentine's Day is confusing. Do I buy Laura jewelry as commercials suggest? Take her out to dinner? Buy her clothes? She's wealthier than I am now – when I inherit my trust fund, it'll add a paltry bit to our joint wealth.

She remains the same – frugal except for paying Jin's tuition, paying Stefan, and paying for the upkeep, all of which Ellen continues to manage. Her clothes remain simple: jeans and tees. There's a good chunk of the money she wishes to donate, she finds the house too big for her taste, and she dislikes the inefficient construction. An idea begins to coalesce.

I find her in the library studying chemistry. She is the most studious girl I know. She's so engrossed in oxidation and reduction processes that she doesn't bother looking up when I enter. It takes a bit to cajole her to our bedroom where I've laid out a dress for her.

It's red. It's silky. It leans toward sexy. I can see the protest on her lips, but her eyes kindle with interest when she examines the dress. A little cajoling occurs on my part, but the final result is worth it. Now that she's filled out, the dress skims her curves softly, leaving just enough to my imagination. I wrap her in a thick wool coat and lead her to my car.

She's quiet and thoughtful during our drive, glancing at me occasionally. I've reserved an entire dining room for us much like I did the day she opened up to me. I show her something on my phone once we're seated.

She peers at it with puzzled interest, her dark eyes taking in the images but not making the connection. "What is this?"

"Our home. Our future home," I amend. "It's not as large as the estate. Smaller. With a guesthouse that can hold Jin and Blake, if they want, or be winterized when not in use. Energy-efficient. Eco-conscious. We can sell the estate and custom-build."

She bites her lower lip as she thinks.

"It's easier to keep secure – we can install security where needed." I don't mention the children's wing that can be added if we need more space.

"A home we design," she breathes, and I can't suppress the satisfaction I feel at her smile.

I gesture one of the servers over to bring the gift I had sent earlier. It's wrapped silvery foil tissue. I want her to rip it open, but she carefully runs a finger where it's secured to remove the wrapping. Her mouth freezes in an open O.

I found a local artist who worked on the painting with me. The image is of a boy and a girl, their silhouettes framed by lights, their bodies leaning in for a kiss while snow falls around them. It's how I remember that February day: the day that I knew Laura would forever hold my heart.

"It's amazing," she whispers, and I can tell from her face that I've nailed it. "Thank you."

I kiss the back of her hand and don't let go until our meal arrives. Her eyes get slightly pensive – I want to know what she's thinking, but I'm worried I won't like the answer.

We return to an unwelcome surprise. I have not seen the shrew in five years, but Hae Atherton remains a beauty. It's a shame she never bent her passions to anything other than herself. She would have been a force to be reckoned with.

Jin is out there, his face flushed with resentment. Laura's father dominated our conversations so much that I've never asked them how they feel about their mother. Five years ago, her affection for her children was minute. She pandered to her oldest: look how handsome, look how strong, look how clever. Her younger children received criticisms: your dress is crooked, comb your hair, be strong like your brother.

My first concern is Laura. I turn to her, ready to do whatever she tells me, but I'm taken aback by the strange impassiveness on her face. She's so still that I come around to help her out of the car, carefully keeping an eye on Hae. Blake and Stefan join us, drawn by the commotion.

Mechanically, Laura hands our painting to Stefan with a whispered request. He nods, but his disgusted sneer at Hae is unmistakable as he heads back into our home.

"I am your mother, Jin! How can you treat me so callously?" Hae exclaims, her face the picture of grief but without the tears. When she sees her daughter – her youngest child – resentment sets her mouth in an ugly line. "And you, Laura! We were promised the money by Clara, and you steal it from us! You are an ungrateful, spoiled child, rotten to the core!"

"That's enough!" I roar, my hands clenched. "You are not to speak to her that way! You are trespassing!"

"Trespassing? To see my children?" she mocks me, her dark red lips curled in disdain. "You are a foolish boy!"

"You can have the money," Laura says in a flat voice, "if you leave us alone."

"No, she can't!" I bark. "I'm your guardian and conservator, and they don't get to bully you to get what they want!"

Laura's dark eyes flicker – I'm already regretting my words. It dismisses and belittles Laura. But Laura moves to her twin's side. I watch them clasp their hands – a united front.

"For years, Father beat me. Beat us." Laura lifts her chin. "You did nothing. You let Brett get away with *everything*. Do you really think I have any compassion for a monster like you?"

Jin continues. "You're not poor. You don't need the damn money. There are people out there more worthy of every penny." He rakes his mother with a glance. "You only care about yourself, but all I see is an ugly woman." Then, with a cruelty so unexpected, he adds, "You're looking old, Mother."

Hae flinches, her lips trembling. It's not from real emotion – she's hurt by the insult. When she glares at her daughter – younger, prettier – it occurs to me that she resents Laura.

"Take a good look at Laura," I say maliciously. "How someone like you gave birth to someone as lovely, as sweet, as good as her is beyond me. She surpasses you in every way."

"I've already called the police." Blake finally speaks, a hint of his former swagger in his voice. "There's a restraining order against you, your husband, and Brett."

"You can't do this!" Hae rages.

"Yes, we can," Laura says, her voice cold. "I'm free of you. Jin is free of you. Go back to that pit of vipers you spawned from. You're dead to me. Now, get off *my* property, you useless bitch, or I'll have you thrown into jail."

The woman shrinks into her diminutive frame, scurrying back to her rental car. I make sure she leaves, alerting our security company to start regular patrols in the area.

Laura retreats to our bedroom, lying on the bed in the red dress and staring at the ceiling blankly. I watch her for a bit, loosening my tie and removing my coat, before sitting beside her. "Ara, are you okay?"

"Yes."

"I'm sorry about snapping earlier. The way I mentioned the guardianship – you have to know that I am not controlling you, Laura." I'm pleading with her because I'm afraid I've pushed her away.

"I know."

I slant my lips to kiss her, running my tongue along the seam of her lips until she parts them for me. Desire, hot and sweet, fills me, and my hand traps her head in place. When my other hand drags her skirt up involuntarily, I feel her tense as usual. I drag my lips away from her reluctantly, standing so my back is to her. She doesn't need to see my frustration. Not now.

"Why do you do that?" she asks.

I'm taking deep breaths, trying to bring myself under control. "Do what?" I sound harsh. I pinch the bridge of my nose.

"Is—something wrong with me?"

Her words shock me so much that I face her in astonishment. "Why would you ask that?"

Her dark eyes are still on the ceiling. "You—always stop. It's like you don't want me."

I'm about to explode. What in the world gave her that idea? "Laura, do you seriously think I don't want you?! You're not here for my personal pleasure! I told you that you control whether or not we have sex."

Her voice drops to a bare whisper. "I've never told you to stop, though."

I'm flabbergasted, but I'm also a few seconds away from hitting my head into a wall. "Laura, you tense up…"

She turns her head to me. "I don't know what to do. I feel as though I should know." Such brutal honesty. "I don't want to do the wrong thing."

Part of me wants to grin. The other part wants to throw a tantrum. I've been playing it too safe. Hardly breathing, I lay down next to her, brushing her lips with my thumb. "Nothing you do could ever be wrong, Ara. I want you. More than anything. Should I show you how much? How far do you want this to go?"

"Show me." The color is high on her cheeks, but her eyes shine at me.

She doesn't need to command me a second time.

CHAPTER 22

Jaylen and Laura dance around each other, blocking jabs and anticipating moves. He stops to point something out, gesturing to her stance which she immediately corrects. After checking her posture, he nods and has her come at him again. Kenji observes, his massive arms crossed over his chest. There are few guys I'd hesitate to fight. Kenji is definitely on the hesitation list. He's a gentle giant, to be sure, but when family and friends are involved? I've never seen anyone more dangerous. Just ask Dario. I'm pretty sure his nose will never look right.

I'm no longer an Idol in the traditional sense. First, I'm married. Second, I don't care about the status anymore. We'll be gone after this year, and it seems as though the school has picked one of their new Idol boys.

That particular, sadly unwary, boy walks in with tousled hair. Jin seems oblivious to the throng of girls who try to impress him. Now that his sister is one of the richest people in town, several girls are hoping to catch his eye. He makes a move with his head, indicating his desire to speak privately.

"What's going on?" I ask, my lips barely moving.

"Brett has left home." His face is rigid with tension. "From what I've heard, he didn't tell my parents."

That's concerning. It's been a few weeks since Hae Atherton showed up. I text our security team – yes, we have one – the details and ask them to check in on Marigold Summers' safety. If we can find her, Brett could, too. I doubt she's his target if he has one. But I'd rather have my bases covered.

Jaylen pivots on his feet, feints, and then jabs sharply. Laura miscalculates and gets struck in the side. I have no recollection of moving. One moment I'm talking to Jin, the next, I see red and I have Jaylen pinned to the floor.

Teeth bared, I'm about to hit him in mindless rage when Laura grabs my clenched hand. "Rory!" she gasps.

The fury dims enough for me to realize what I'm doing. Jaylen's face is turned like he's waiting for the hit to land. "Sorry," I mutter, letting him go.

"When I agreed to help, I knew the risks," Jaylen says, making me feel that much worse.

I help him stand before examining my wife. "It'll hardly bruise," she grumps when I run my fingers over the spot. I won't tell her about Brett. Not yet. We don't know anything; for all we know, Brett is on the run or doing something psychotic.

Even as I think that, I know I'm wrong. A guy willing to drop his twelve-year-old sister doesn't run. He plows over people with complete disregard. He attacked Marigold Summers probably to see if he could get away with it. Lionel Atherton was complicit in the crime, hiding the evidence and framing my brother, to protect his favored son.

It's a myth that psychopathic people who hurt and kill want to be caught. The truth is that they don't believe they can be caught. That's Brett in a nutshell. Whether he was born that way or created by his abnormal parents is unknown.

"Can we ask Stefan to make pizza?" Laura asks, breaking into my grim thoughts by clasping her arms around my neck. "Gooey, cheesy pizza with mushrooms. Lots of mushrooms."

Jin adds, "With bell peppers."

Both Jaylen and I groan. The twins glare in offense. What's wrong with pepperoni? I have Jin call Stefan and give him the requests while Laura packs her things up.

"When I take Laura to Bora Bora, it'll be Blake, Jin, and Stefan at the house. Brett's on the loose." I don't say anything more. Jaylen knows the details.

Jaylen's father owns a security firm – it does everything from mall security to personal security. If money is not an issue, you can hire some pretty brutal people to protect you. "I'll have Dad put an extra detail on your home," he says immediately. His family did the new security system, and they'll do the security at the place we're building.

"I want that douchebag taken care of," I hiss, watching Laura and Emily tease Kenji about something.

Jaylen smirks. "Well, gee, Rory, I'm not sure if I can arrange a hit." He becomes serious quickly. "Take your girl to Bora Bora. I'll hold things down here. I'll keep them safe."

"Thanks." I exhale slowly.

CHAPTER 23

To make up for our hasty wedding and lack of wooing, I spend our entire honeymoon sweeping my wife off her feet. I worship her, take her for romantic walks, and we make love under the stars and to the sound of the waves.

What does Laura do? She brings her homework. My girl brings her homework along on our honeymoon. I want to get upset, but she's so damn adorable writing out her pH problems that I decide the only thing to do is punish her. Her punishment is unending distractions – kisses, massages, and a whole host of other tortures. She doesn't complain, so, clearly, I'm doing it right.

Her body is soft and relaxed as we land at the small airport. "I think I like being married to you, Rory," she whispers.

"Good. I lied about willingly giving you a divorce if you wanted it. I planned on begging, pleading, and chaining myself to your leg if you asked for one."

"Hmmm. Maybe I'll ask for one just to see that." Her lashes flutter at me teasingly right before I kiss her.

I'm reluctant to end the kiss, but we need to get off the plane. "I'll beg you tonight if you want," I murmur in her ear, pulling back to see her blush. "I love you so much, Ara." I can't help my declaration.

If there's only one kink in our relationship, it's that she's never said the same thing to me. I think she loves me. And yet, I don't want to ask her outright out of fear.

The car we hired to pick us up waits right outside the terminal, the driver coming out to grab our bags. I cup Laura's face in the cold wind, intending to steal one last kiss before we head home, when she gasps as she's pulled from me.

Everything moves both too fast and too slow. Me realizing too late the driver is Brett. Brett pressing a gun to Laura. Laura freezing when she realizes who has her. Me moving to hit Brett only to stop when I see the gun digging into her side.

If you take Jin and gave him a deranged look, that would sum up Brett. His eyes are huge in his grinning face. "Hello, sister," he says right in her ear. "You've been a naughty girl. Very naughty." He looks at me. "I want you to back up and walk right into the building. Or my sweet sister gets a new hole as a wedding present. Is she still sweet, Remington?"

I won't let him satisfy his perversions. "You're planning on killing her, aren't you?" My voice is surprisingly calm.

"Kill her? No. I'd never kill my sweet sister." Laura's eyes widen in horror, and I wonder if he's said something similar to her before. "She's coming with me. She'll take care of me, won't you, Laura? Banish my fevers and make me soup."

"Yes, Brett, I'll take care of you," Laura says, her eyes meeting mine. "We can go."

"No." The word escapes my mouth before I can stop myself.

The gun digs in harshly, and Laura closes her eyes. I back off, moving away. Maybe he won't kill her, and I need to take that risk because he'll shoot her if I try anything else. Her dark eyes shine at me, but as I open my mouth to say something, I notice her finger lightly tap her jacket. Her phone. She has her phone in her pocket. She's telling me to use the phone to track her.

"I love you, Laura," I say as her brother moves her back towards the car.

"I love you, too," she says, and I want to rage.

This is not how I wanted to learn she loves me! And I know she says it now, thinking this may be our last time together. My hands clench and I have to fight every cell in my body to not make a run for her. Brett smiles, opening the door and shoving her in, before getting in beside her. I'm already moving as I see him push her into the driver's seat.

The moment the car peels off, I rage, falling to my knees and hitting the cold ground. I think I scream. And then I'm on the phone with Jaylen, nearly shouting the details with a mix of fear for Laura and helpless anger. The news he gives me is terrifying. Two days ago, authorities think Brett threw acid on his mother and killed his father. Hae Atherton is alive, in the hospital, scarred for life. Lionel Atherton is dead.

What does this mean for Laura? From all accounts, Brett was doted on by his parents – they covered for him, they hurt people for him.

But I'm not allowed to expose my legs or wear anything too tight. He's been like that since the incident. I think it's to protect me from Brett, to be honest.

Laura's words haunt me. What if – what if her father had been trying to protect her in his sick way? Protect himself? Give his eldest child, one he could never control, just enough power to think he could do as he pleased. A monster and a sadist. I shudder. Laura. A sadist has my Laura.

By the time Jaylen reaches me at the airport, his father is tracking Laura's cell. We don't call the police. I know better than that.

"Jin," I gasp, reaching my brother-in-law.

"I know," he says, his voice dull. "He already called me."

"Are you in a car? What the hell are you doing?!" I shout at him.

"I'm going to save my sister. They're heading to the school." He hangs up on me.

I turn to Jaylen, pale. What the hell?

CHAPTER 24

"We should wait here until the team shows up," Jaylen advises, his face tight with worry.

"I'm not waiting," I snarl.

I see the car and the Range Rover. Jin got here first. Shit. I'm not waiting.

Jaylen just looks at me, measuring me. "I'll wait for the team."

Jaylen's father speaks to us over the phone. "Buy us time, Rory. The team is on its way. Get him to talk. Try and get some distance between her and Brett."

The air is bitter outside, but the wind doesn't blow. A recent dusting of snow allows me to track the footprints. I see Laura's smaller ones, smudged as if she stumbled or was being dragged, next to bigger ones. And then other steps behind that – as if Jin was following carefully, cautiously.

Across the courtyard, into the fields behind the school. And then I hear voices.

"So, what's the plan, Brett?" Jin's voice is calm but wary.

I slide along the edge of the building and peek around. On the edge of a small pond, now frozen over, Brett holds Laura by the arm. The gun presses into her side. She doesn't seem scared, her eyes pinned to her twin's face.

Brett lets out this weird laugh. "I'm not sure. I thought – I had a plan, you know."

Jin slides a little closer. "I don't think you hate us. I don't think you hate Laura."

Laura's breath comes out in faint huffs. "Brett." She says his name. Her voice doesn't tremble. Good girl. Brett feeds off fear. "You killed Father." Her face turns to him. "Thank you."

I'll be honest, I didn't see those words coming. But it's the perfect thing to say. Some of the mania leaves Brett's face as he regards his sister. "Oh, he knew," Brett says with a cruel chuckle. "He knew when I killed him that he was never in control of me." He does this creepy thing where he rubs his face against Laura's. For a moment, revulsion crosses her face before she blanks completely. "I'm pleased with Mom's punishment, too."

I go around the edge of the building so that I can get closer to Jin from the back of the building. Jin can see me if he turns sideways, but he continues to stare ahead. From my vantage point, I might be able to reach Jin in about five to six seconds.

"It's a bit of a mess, Brett. What happens now?" Jin's hands go in his pockets like he's on a casual stroll.

"We could start fresh," Laura suggests. "Find a place – a quiet place – to settle."

"No," Brett says grimly, his eyes growing wild. "You ruined it, Laura. You had to marry that guy. Why would you do that?"

The twins continue to look at each other. "Laura's my twin. I'm not abandoning her," Jin interrupts. "What are you going to do to her?"

"I know you're fucking twins," Brett snaps. "Dad gave me Marigold, but that's not who I wanted."

Laura's eyes close as a sick feeling overwhelms me. I can see it now: Brett torn between his unnatural, unholy desires, and his rage. His violence against his sister, his need to control her and subdue her. He may have even planted the thoughts of taking away her rights in their father.

"Dad lost control of Laura, so I had to fix it," Brett adds, shaking his head.

"I'll go with you wherever you want." Laura keeps her voice calm and reasonable. Only the faint wrinkle on her forehead belies her true state. She's trying to understand if Brett is going to kill her or keep her.

"That's the problem," Brett says, shaking his head. "It doesn't work that way." He stares at his younger brother with a frown. "You're not broken. You'll run, Laura."

"No, I won't. We can walk away from this together."

I realize sooner than Laura that he doesn't want her this way, standing and reasonable. He wants her unable to function.

I move at the same time the gun moves to point at Jin. Brett sees me, but Laura's pushing his arm so that the shot he fires misses her twin. He slips and falls, taking Laura with him. Her hand flies out, fingers curved, as she rakes them down her brother's face before slamming the heel of her hand at his nose. She doesn't have enough momentum to do significant damage, but it's enough for his hold to loosen so they're briefly parted.

I'm a second or two away – too far – as Brett realizes what's happening and the gun swings towards Laura. My heart stops as a shot cracks through the air, Laura falling as my fingers reach her. I'm pulling her to me, my brain screaming, and we tumble together.

"No!" I scream, my eyes frantically searching Laura's shocked face and body for injuries. I find none and my eyes go to Brett.

He's lying face up, hands outstretched, his eyes blank, his face relaxed. Dead, he looks slightly angelic. Only the blood seeping onto the ground, the bits of brain matter, the hole in the front of his head, give testimony.

Jin reaches us a second later, but my arms won't let Laura go, so he's forced to embrace both of us as Jaylen comes running. In the distance, I see a man holding a type of rifle with a scope. But my brain won't function beyond thinking, *She's safe. She's safe.*

CHAPTER 25

Laura sleeps, her twin beside her, for the entire day. I manage to deal with the questions, the police, the FBI, and the lawyers. Stefan pushes soup on me, Blake hovers with worry, my parents fuss over me. Jaylen and Zyair hang around for emotional support. At the end of the day, I kick Jin out of my bed and take my wife in my arms.

I'm not glad that Brett and Lionel are dead. We should never wish for death. But I am glad that I won't have to worry about them haunting us anymore. Laura's mother will be taken care of. It's more than she deserves. All the family's remaining wealth went to Jin and Laura equally, but Jin will handle the estate details.

"When will school be over?" Jin groans over a week later.

My mother is a terror on the phone, but there's only so much she can get us excused from classes.

"We're done at the very end of May," Laura states reasonably. "You only have two more months."

I park the car in the lot, letting Jin hand me my backpack before giving Laura a hand out of the car. She doesn't need a hand, of course. I just like doing it.

Jin grumps to himself as we walk together to join Jaylen and Zyair inside the cafeteria. Emily and Kenji join us a few minutes later, and I evaluate our hodgepodge group that's formed. I walk Laura to class, lingering by the door to snag a few kisses, before Emily shouts, "For God's sake, you'll be fine not kissing her every five minutes."

I flip Emily off, which she returns, and head to class. I wonder if that thrill of being with Laura will ever leave. Is that what happens with old married couples?

I take the long way to math class – it happens to take me right by Laura's chemistry class. As I round the corner, I can't mistake the ringing voice of Paris Dumonte. I stop and back up before either Paris or Laura notice me.

"Now I know why he married you," she sneers loudly. "Killed your aunt, did you, to get all the money?"

The media has had a field day with the Athertons. Speculation on whether Clara Atherton was murdered remains. It wouldn't surprise me if either Lionel or Brett killed her. With her body being cremated, we'll probably never know.

"Just know that every time he screws you, I had him first," Paris adds harshly.

I decide that's enough, my hands ready to take control of the situation. But Laura's soft voice stops me. "I'm sorry you feel that way and that you're upset," she says far too kindly. "Have you considered counseling? It's worked wonders for me."

I move into plain sight, and Laura's dark eyes meet mine. "Is there a problem?" I purr in a dangerous tone.

Paris jumps, her eyes widening.

"Paris was just stopping to say she might seek counseling," Laura says blithely. She extends her hand to me. "Did you come the long way just to walk with me?"

I grin. "Yes."

We leave Paris behind us.

After school, we stop by the site where we're building our new home. It's too cold to start any of the real work, but I meet with the contractors and architect to discuss the plan. As we analyze the terrain, Laura walks with Jin, both bundled in thick coats.

While they walk, the twins whisper to each other. I swear they're talking in code. It's private. I never pry or ask questions. They've been through so much. I realize that I'd hinged my college decisions based on Laura's desires, but hers will hinge on her brother's.

"It'll be a good place for a home," Jin says, his voice clear now that he's addressing me. "Laura wants a sauna."

"I know, I know." I've already worked that in.

Laura's making a massive donation to survivors of abuse once she turns eighteen, a decision I fully support. I've had our lawyers working on removing the guardianship and conservatorship. No one will take away her right to independence ever again.

When we reach home, Laura checks her messages and I see the faint frown on her face. "What is it?" I ask.

"Marigold Summers. She received my letter."

Laura, in lieu of a phone call, had written a long letter to Marigold Summers.

"What does she say?" I ask as Blake listens on.

"She said she always knew it wasn't Blake," Laura says quietly. "And she thanked me for telling her the truth."

I wonder if that knowledge is what prevented Marigold from pressing charges. "It's over. Let's put the past behind us," I say, including Blake with my eyes.

Laura's lost in her memories as she stares out the window. "Yes, let's," she agrees.

EPILOGUE

5 years later....

Laura's on her phone talking to an event coordinator for the charity ball she's hosting in a week when I get home. After graduating from high school, Laura decided to launch her own foundation. I continued on to college after taking a gap year. Jin and I chose the same college. He starts medical school this year.

When Laura sees me, her face lights up as she ends her call. Even after five years, I still get a thrill when she smiles at me. Now that summer's about to begin, I intend to make the most of my time with my wife.

"We sold out on tickets," she tells me before kissing me. "I think we'll outdo last year's fundraising."

"After this, let's take a break where we can be alone," I suggest.

She lifts a delicate brow. "I have something to tell you, but I'm worried the timing is bad."

I'm immediately on alert. "What's wrong? Did something happen? Are you unwell?" I think about the past few days. Now that I think about it, she hasn't been eating very much.

Her eyes lower, her lashes fanning her cheeks. "I'm pregnant."

I go completely still. "Ara," I whisper. "Are you sure?"

"Are you unhappy?"

How could she ask that? I swing her up in my arms. "You need to get off your feet." I rush her to our bedroom, climbing the steps two at a time.

"Rory, what the hell? I'm pregnant, not sick, you oaf!" Laura's face flushes with annoyance.

I gently deposit her on the bed. "You've been feeling sickly, haven't you? You need to take it easy and not stress so much. I'll talk to Ellen and have her help with the ball."

Laura scowls. "If you fuss too much, you'll make your wife very unhappy." She pauses, pulling at my tie a little. "How do you feel about this?"

Laura knows I hate to see her in pain or discomfort. The thought of her undergoing labor terrifies me. I want children, but I can't bear the thought that selfishness on my part might cause her pain. "Scared. Happy. Ara, you know how I am when it comes to you. I don't want you to hurt." I kiss her cheek, gently holding my body above hers so I don't squish her. "I'll be at every doctor visit, every test." Reverently, I press a kiss to her stomach. "Our child, Ara." I look up at her in awe, the reality hitting me hard. "I love you."

With an impish smile, she yanks at my tie to lure me back to her lips. "Show me," she whispers.

I do exactly that.

ACKNOWLEDGEMENT

To my game friends: Celest, Anchor, Arranis, Mael, AegentEight, Occisor, Feeeg, Luckette, AndLee, Zero, Rozz, CowboyJBB, Zilt, Quinni, Rilf, happyreader, Rigel, RMB, RM, chaotic, DOE, Drifter, Pinkle, rum, brewer, Unicorn, Chewy, Batchick, Fire Oni, and many others.

Thank you for listening, supporting, and letting me be my silly self.

Thank you for encouraging me to write.

Thank you for helping me when I messed up with my gear in game.

ABOUT THE AUTHOR

L J Byrne

LJ Byrne considers herself an engineer by education, a writer by heart, and a general know-it-all when it comes to strange and useless information. She won her first writing award at 21 and then never published or wrote again for over two decades. When her essay describing her experiences with post-partum depression was selected for Listen  to Your Mother Twin Cities, the writing bug hit her again. Her writing style is diverse and the only thing she can't do is philosophize. She lives in the Twin Cities with her husband, her two sons, her beloved bunnies, and a very fluffy cat.

BOOKS BY THIS AUTHOR

Survivor

www.ingramcontent.com/pod-product-compliance
Lightning Source LLC
Chambersburg PA
CBHW020743160726
47993CB00006B/2584